And So On...

THE BAREBACK ANTHOLOGY

BareBackPress

This is a work of fiction. The characters, incidents, and dialogue are the products of the author's imagination and are not to be construed as real. Any resemblance to actual events or person, living or dead, is entirely coincidental.

BareBackPress
Hamilton, Ontario, Canada
For enquiries visit www.barebackpress.com
Cover photo, layout and design by Peter Jelen

And So On...And Son On...And So On... And So On...And So
On... And So On...And Son On...And So On... And So On...And
So On...And So On...And Son On...And So On... And So
On...And So On...And So On...And Son On...And So On... And
So On...And So On...And So On...And Son On...And So On...
And So On...And So On...And So On...And Son On...And So
On... And So On...And So On...And So On...And Son On...And
So On... And So On...And So On...And So On...And Son
On...And So On... And So On...And So On...And So On...And
Son On...And So On... And So On...And So On...And So
On...And Son On...And So On... And So On...And So On...And
So On...And Son On...And So On... And So On...And So
On...And So On...And Son On...And So On... And So On...And
So On...And So On...And Son On...And So On... And So
On...And So On...And So On...And Son On...And So On... And
So On...And So On...And So On...And Son On...And So On...
And So On...And So On... And So On...And Son On...And So
On... And So On...And So On...And So On...And Son On And
So On... And So On...And So On...And So On...And Son
On...And So On... And So On...And So On...And So On...And
Son On...And So On... And So On...And So On...And So
On...And Son On...And So On... And So On...And So On...And
So On...And Son On...And So On... And So On...And So On...
And So On...And Son On...And So On... And So On...And So
On...And So On...And Son On...And So On... And So On...And
So On...And So On...And Son On...And So On... And So
On...And So On... And So On...And Son On...And So On... And
So On...And So On...And So On...And Son On...And So On...
And So On...And So On...And So On...And Son On...And So
On... And So On...And So On...And So On...And Son On...And
So On... And So On...And So On...And So On...And Son
On...And So On... And So On...And So On...And So On...And
Son On...And So On... And So On...And So On...And So
On...And Son On...And So And So On...And So On...And So
On...And Son On...And So On... And So On...And So On...And
So On...And Son On...And So On... And So On...And So On...
And So On...And Son On...And So On... And So On...And So
On... And So On...And Son On...And So On... And So On...And
So On...And So On...And Son On...And So On... And So
On...And So On...And So On...And Son On...And So On... And
So On...And So On...And So On...And Son On...And So On...
And So On...And So On...And So On...And Son On...And So
On... And So On...And So On... And So On...And Son On......

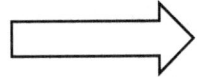

AND SO ON...

Mother's Day
Arthur Graham

Norman Mailer once said, "Writing books is the closest men ever come to childbearing." And here I was thinking the closest we ever came was taking a massive shit. Same thing for some, I guess.

I close my laptop and set it on the table in front of me, nodding to the barista behind the counter as I rise to collect my things. It is Mother's Day, incidentally, and I'm off to mail a card that's going to be late enough already as it is.

I've almost made it to my car when I'm accosted by a pair of young women, ostensibly in their early twenties, though looking much physically older. Judging from their dirty clothes, stringy hair, and sickly pallor, these gals have clearly made some poor life choices.

"Excuse me mister," one of them begins, "my sister and I are stranded, and we're trying to get bus fare. Do you think maybe you could help us out?"

The talker isn't much to look at, but her sister is all right, at least in a snaggletoothed meth head kind of way.

"You girls mothers?" I ask, looking them up and down.

"Huh?" They look confusedly at each other.

"Never mind," I say. "Well, you at least *have* a mother, right?"

"Ummm, sure mister," the less-awful one replies. "Do you have any spare change? Anything helps."

"I think I can probably do you better than that on Mother's Day," I say, digging out my wallet and leafing through the bills. "How'd you girls like to make a quick twenty?"

They look at each other, then at me in disbelief.

"Twenty dollars each?!"

"No, you get to split it."

They shoot each other another quick glance. "Okay, sure!"

"Get in the car."

I've been living in this town for years now, and if there was one thing I've learned, it's this: Nobody gives head like a meth head, if only because they're always either completely cranked or just desperate to get there, all drool and whiplash as both a means and an end to the next hit. It is a simple fact of commerce that these people will do just about anything to get you fixed and themselves fixed in the process, and I am but an innocent bystander to the economic realities of that whole situation.

If it hadn't been me, it would've been some other perv they landed.

When the older sister finally comes up for air, I grab the younger one by the hair and really let her tonsils have it.

"Your mother would be *soooo* proud," I say to her as she chokes the whole thing down.

I'm so into fucking her throat that I don't even notice the knife coming up against my own.

I feel the exquisite sting of air as my neck opens up to the outside world, the blade slicing clean across as my blood begins to spill.

My murderer rifles through my pockets while her sister obliviously continues her task, blowing me as if her own life depended on it.

I thought that was awfully nice of them, finishing me off in both ways.

Honestly, I don't know how I'm able to keep any blood in my cock with how much of it I've lost at this point, but at any rate, somehow I always knew it would end this way.

Finally, I blow my load and die.

My last thoughts are naturally with my mother.

With All My Faculties
Arthur Graham

It started like any other day, which is to say I woke up, got dressed, and went out to take Billy for a walk.

Based on available context, you'd probably guess that Billy is my dog, or my frog, or perhaps my hog, like one of those cute little pigs people keep instead of eating, but no, you'd be wrong on either count.

Neither is Billy a baboon, a bassoon, or a balloon.

Balloons don't walk, they float, and while it is indeed possible to take one's bass for a walk, at least in terms of musical parlance, the bassoon is in fact another type of instrument altogether. Baboons can't really be said to walk either, they more or less just amble about, but now I'm officially getting off track.

You see, in all actuality, Billy is my Conscience.

I know, you're probably thinking "aha! What he's really saying is that he took *his cricket* for a walk," but no, you're being too figurative now. Aside from the fact that crickets do a lot more hopping than walking, it is also worth remembering that I am not Pinocchio, therefore my Conscience is not represented by a walking, talking bug.

No, as strange as it sounds, I took my literal Conscience for a walk.

Sometimes, when things are weighing on my Conscience, I like to take it on long, brisk strolls around the park. Helps to shed those extra pounds. It is usually best to exercise Billy like this first thing in the morning, making room for all the weight he's sure to accumulate before the end of the day.

On this particular day, we run into Frank, my Imagination, at the park where we like to go walking.

"Hello Frank," I say to my Imagination, who has stopped to do some stretching by the path.

"What the fuck," Frank says, touching his toes. "Forget about the restraining order already?"

"Hmmm..." I reply, genuinely unsure. "Perhaps you could jog my Memory?"

"Karl went off ahead," Frank says, rising straight. "You may not remember, but we will never forget what you did to Amy!"

And with that, he is gone, leaving just the vaguest recollection of Reason in his wake.

"Well," I say to Billy, who has already doubled in size, "guess we're doing extra laps today...."

It's Alright
Arthur Graham

It is before first period at Bayside High, and as part of their inaugural "Cruelty-Free Friday", the gang has volunteered to cook a vegan breakfast for their fellow schoolmates. For some reason, they have set up their cooking line by the lockers in the hall, as opposed to in the cafeteria.

Mr. Belding walks up and admires the students hard at work, fondly reminiscing on his own vegan youth. While he distracts them with a story about how cool he used to be, surviving on hummus and couscous all throughout college, the tofu scramble begins to burn.

Smoke fills the hall, and Zack struggles to scrape the blackened slop off the griddle. Jessie flees in frustration, Slater goes to grab a fire extinguisher, and Kelly resumes filing her nails. Screech is just being Screech.

When zombies suddenly overrun the school, it's like the last thing they need on this disastrous Cruelty-Free Friday. Are they allowed to be cruel in self-defense? Does it count if the animals are already dead?

Larry, the paraplegic gun nut student, has the answer.

While many of the extras and several of the minor characters are devoured by invading zombies, he wheels on over to his locker and yells for everyone to follow him. Distributing the arsenal of AR-15s he keeps hidden inside, he finds with some dismay that he is fresh out of bullets since his last school shooting. He asks Zack to run out and get some 5.56mm ammunition, but Zack is currently running the pancake station.

Zack asks Larry why he can't run out for ammo himself. Larry points to his crippled legs and explains that he can't run out for anything because he cannot run. Zack asks Slater if he can run out in his stead, but Slater doesn't hear him, because he is too busy making out with Max, owner of The Max diner, against a nearby locker. With few options left, Zack leaves all cooking duties to Screech and makes a break for the gun store across the street.

Screech proves surprisingly adept at running the breakfast line all by himself, calmly flipping almond milk pancakes and meatless sausage patties while zombies bash against the windows and the doors of the school. But he is hungry, and cannot wait for the meal to be served, and so he sneaks a surreptitious snap of the Slim Jim in his back pocket.

Catching him in the act as she walks past, Jessie glares at him, turns around, and stomps off in a huff, swearing to herself that she will never sleep with the carnivorous Screech again.

Just as the massive horde of zombies breach their defenses and pour into the school, Zach returns with armloads of ammo, breathlessly distributing boxes of 7.62mm rounds to the students.

Everyone loads up, takes aim, and dies from the shrapnel of a dozen exploding rifles.

ARTHUR GRAHAM is a professional editor, writer, and book critic currently residing in Salt Lake City, Utah. He is an accomplished noveler, storyist, and publishite by all accounts. His work has been unfairly compared to that of Charles Bukowski, William S. Burroughs, Hunter S. Thompson, and Kurt Vonnegut, Jr. Once a promising purveyor of fine literary fiction, he has since been reduced to churning out zines instead. He is not on Facebook but he does own a TV, so at least he's not a total hipster. Cofounder and former head editor of Rooster Republic Pres

homicide
Kurt Nimmo

the bullet
entered his chest
half way up.
he was standing
near the open window
of the car
when the rifle
was fired.
the bullet traveled
through him
at an angle and exited
at the top of his head.
it blew off
the top of his skull.
a second shot
was fired before
the man hit the ground
and this shot was centered
directly above
where the first shot had struck.
both shots
left punctures
resembling knife wounds.
the holes
pinched inward
from the force of the bullets.
he was already
turning blue
when I walked over
after parking my car
along the opposite curb.
an old woman
came out of her house.
she said the man
lived down the street
and people were afraid of him.

he was a violent drunk.
the whole family was no good
the old woman said.
the man
was walking back
from the liquor store when
a green station wagon
pulled up and words were exchanged
and then two shots fired.
she saw
the muzzle flashes
and thought somebody
was playing with fire crackers
inside the car.
then the man fell
in the driveway of the house
across from where
I rented an upstairs flat.
the green station wagon
moved off at a normal speed
as if nothing had happened.
the old woman
told me all of this
from the middle of the street.
she would not
look at the dead guy
sprawled out
with a pint of cheap vodka
in a brown paper bag
beside his head.
later a neighbor said
the dead guy
had messed around
with some other guy's wife.
I stood on the opposite curb as
a crowd gathered. a woman shrieked
and another one cried
and then the cops
showed up.
a homicide detective

dressed like a homicide detective
on a 70s television show
asked me a few questions
and I told him
what I saw.
he scribbled something
in a blue notebook with
DETROIT POLICE
stenciled on the front
and then
he walked off.
I stood there
smoking a cigarette
and thought
it might
be a good idea
to move
out of
that neighborhood.

Fleas
Kurt Nimmo

earlier my wife
went across the street
to see the neighbor's new kitten.
when she came back
she said the little guy has fleas.
so now I sit here
before the machine and think
fleas are biting me.
there is something crawling on my elbow.
I stop writing
and examine my elbow.
nothing there.
well, fleas are small. you can miss them.
then it's my ankle, so I raise my leg
and pull up the cuff of my pants and twist my leg
looking for parasites.
damn it.
I go back to clacking on the keyboard.
then it's my neck.
I scratch there until it
feels like I've ripped the skin off.
I think about taking a bath.
I think about pouring gasoline in there.
it would not be wise to do this.
it would be stupid
and might not kill the fleas.
fleas have me thinking like an idiot.
I jump up out of the chair and go to the window.
I look out the window
and see the woman across the street.
she's on the lawn with the kitten.
the kitten jumps up and down
and the woman jumps up and down.
they're having a lot of fun
while I'm in misery.
I figure she must have

passed all the fleas on to my wife
and they are happy and flea-free over there.
I go back and sit down at the machine.
suddenly there is
an itch in my arm pit.
I shove a finger in there
and wiggle it around.
I can't write.
I can't do anything.
there's a bottle of scotch in the kitchen cabinet.
I think it will solve
my problem or it will at least
make it more likely I do not care
if there are fleas crawling
all over me
like a hungry army
or if it is my imagination
working in over-
drive again.

KURT NIMMO born in Detroit, Michigan in 1952. In the late '70s, he co-edited the successful literary magazine, The Smudge. In the '80s, he edited Planet Detroit. He currently edit Busted Dharma, an online poetry magazine. Kurt has been nominated for several Pushcart Prizes for fiction, and two of his books were selected as "modern classics" by the Wormwood Review. He lives in Texas with his wife and two cats.

Boarderline Whiner
J. Tarwood

I've never been enchanted
by life, blue butterfly fanning
a black turd. Boo-hoo,
boo-hoo: I learned little
I'm not one of you.
Popped from a senile womb,
I picked up yearning,
Sahara seed
dreaming out its drought.

For lack of an off button,
I dabbled with pills
and dawdled with razors.
Body always balked, bewildered bronco,
spooked by perfect black.
I used to then make believe
till I believed
in a big country elsewhere,
elegant kissing, electric talking,
everybody just true
as the best words
in a bold book.

My ashes, maybe, will figure out the way.

Learning To Swallow
J. Tarwood

Mom can whisper.
Snoring in rocker,
Daddy mustn't know.
Her breasts shove my fingers.
Her breath stains mine.
Daddy's a tired man.
He'd never understand.

I gulp everything down.
There's a burning
like gargled vinegar.
I gulp that down too.

Awake, Daddy sniffs.
He'll die dumb.
It's all buried in my belly
like cocaine in a condom.

J. TARWOOD has been a dishwasher, a community organizer, a medical archivist, a documentary film producer, an oral historian, and a teacher. Much of his life has been spent in East Africa, Latin America, and the Middle East. He has published three books, *And For The Mouth A Flower*, *Grand Detour* and *The Cats In Zanzibar*, and his poems have appeared in magazines ranging from *American Poetry Review* to *Visions*. He has always been an unlikely man in unlikely places.

Soul Cancer
Matthew J. Hall

I have this guilt in the pit of my stomach; a sickness. It's like a ball of milk and cheese perpetually souring. It shrinks and grows according to occasion. As a child I would lock myself in the bathroom and cry big, clear, silent tears. Those are the type I sobbed today. If it weren't so fucking tragic it would be comical.

Earlier in the day I told a street fundraiser I had cancer so she'd leave me alone. She had done that slow-motion-jogging-backwards thing when I tried to walk past her. She was letting me know through body language that she's fun and easy going, smiling like we were old friends. I don't even like talking to people I know; once I get past the usual pleasantries I'm lost. So when it comes to strangers who want me to take part in a fun-time chat, I'm fucked. But I couldn't help feeling sorry for her. The rejection of it all is so overwhelming. One dismissal after another. It's got to be exhausting. Having all those smiles wiped away by stone-cold refusals. It's like I have these two contrasting urges: anxiety wanted me to tell her to fuck off and die in a cold and lonely room, while empathy insisted I set up a direct debit, cuddle her in close, stroke her hair and tell her, "Everything will be okay."

She was pretty. She had these crooked front teeth and a slight lisp, crimped hair and green eyes. I imagined us married and almost happy. I imagined her coming home from a hard day of saving the whale, or the environment, or whatever noble cause she'd been assigned on that particular day - one direct debit at a time - tired and dejected. I'd rub her shoulders with oil and just listen. I'd let her rant as much as she needed, let her use me as an emotional punch bag. I'd soak up all the rejection from every one of those assholes who wouldn't respond to her backwards-jogging-fun-time-chat. Then I imagined her going too far: accusing my massage technique of making her feel worse, raising her voice, pointing out that I didn't understand what it was like to stand out there in the cold with a shit-eating grin plastered all over my face day after day. She'd call me "pathetic" and "worthless cunt". She'd be picking a fight so she wouldn't feel quite so bad when she finally plucked up the courage to confess.

'I'm leaving you for your brother.'

I pictured myself not knowing what to say or do, so I just keep on rubbing her shoulders. She's pretty tense so I add a little pressure. I press my thumbs in a firm, circular motion around the knots.

'Aren't you going to say anything?' She says.

'You are very tense.' I say.

'What?'

'Your shoulders are tenser than ever.' I say, changing the circular motion to more of an up and down type of affair.

'Did you hear what I said?'

'You're leaving me for my brother.' I confirmed.

I imagined her breaking away from the massage and standing over me. She's offended by my lack of reaction. And rightly so. After all, she is my wife and he is my brother and they have been fucking. And she's been comparing our moves and penis sizes. And he probably gives better massages than I do. And she gives him head. And he goes down on her. And she lets him spank her. And they do role-play. And they fuck outside. And he understands the erogenous zones. And he isn't mystified by female genitalia. He never fumbles around wondering if he's found "it" or not. And she's faked every orgasm I ever thought I'd given her. Oh God. She's right. I am a worthless cunt. Of course she's fucking my brother. I can't blame her for that. I brought the whole thing on myself. She deserves to be happy. I'll sign the divorce papers and be my brother's best man.

It was at that point in my daydream when she started to slowly jog backwards and give me that long-lost-friend smile.

'Hiya,' she said. 'You look like a fun guy. Can you spare five minutes?'

We both knew I didn't look like a fun guy. I look like I'm either going to finally crack, pull out a concealed weapon and start ruthlessly taking out men, women and children before turning the weapon on myself, or, curl up into the foetal position, rock back and forth steadily and sob freely.

'I promise it'll only take five minutes.'

I decided there and then not to believe a single word she said. I kept walking. She kept backwards jogging.

'I'm just inviting people like yourself to chat for five minutes.' She said, still smiling and still backwards jogging. She's quite good at it. It was like she had eyes in the back of her head.

'Just five minutes.' She assured me, as if five minutes didn't mean anything. But I knew what it could lead to. I knew I couldn't trust her; that we could potentially fall in love, and the love could run dry and she could fuck my brother.

'I can't stop. I'm late for work.'

I wondered how much longer she could keep jogging blind before she tripped or bumped into an oncoming pedestrian. I wondered what type of sound her skull would make as it cracked open on the pavement. I saw myself kneeling in a puddle of her blood, holding her twitching body in my arms, looking up to the heavens and shouting at God for his spite and cruelty.

'Nobody has spoken to me today and I think I'm going to get fired.' She said.

Such manipulation. I had to get away.

'I have cancer.' I blurted. We both stopped dead in our tracks.

'Oh my God. I am so sorry.' She stared at me, sad and true, genuinely sorry for me.

'Yeah I'm pretty much going to be dead very soon so I can't really think about setting up any standing orders right now.'

'I'm so sorry. That's awful.' she said.

I could see tears beginning to well in her eyes. This wasn't how it was supposed to play out. She was supposed to move onto the next rube. I wasn't supposed to be the last straw on the fundraiser's back.

'It's testicular.' I said, hoping that would kill the conversation once and for all.

'Oh my God.' she said, tears rolling down her face.

The rejection, the loss, the death of hope and all her anguish suddenly rose to the surface. I could see all her pain spilling out right in front of me and in that moment, I too, was swept away by a strange, shared pain.

She threw her arms around me, cuddled me in close, stroked my hair and told me everything would be okay. And we stood like that for five minutes, both of us embracing the other, and crying big, clear, silent tears.

MATTHEW J. HALL is a UK writer based in Bristol. His poetry chapbook, Pigeons and Peace Doves is available through Blood Pudding Press. He reviews small press books at www.screamingwithbrevity.com

Tinnitus
Kyle Heger

I hate it when doctors call what I got tinnitus. It reminds me too much of the first time I heard that damn poem. The bells. I was in high school. Some old bat of a teacher was going on and on about how that poet with the weird-ass face who fell in love with his own 13-year old cousin made up a word. Tintinnabulation. Like we was supposed to be impressed or something. She practically drove me crazy talking about the creative temperament and the subconscious and roots of words. Yeah. Right. Like words really have roots. Long, bloody roots, like the roots of teeth.

I told the guy next to me I could make up words too. I told him I had a bad case of whothefuckcaresitis.

The old bat heard me and asked if I had something to contribute to the class discussion.

So I repeated what I said.

She pretended not to hear me that time. She kind of pushed those tiny little glasses back up her nose without looking at me. I was not someone you wanted to mess with even in those days. I was trouble.

If you knew me, you would know I am not the kind of guy who usually pays a lot of attention to poems. But for some reason that thing really got to me. It sank its teeth in me. Teeth with long bloody roots. Some parts of it I did not get. Some of the words did not make sense, some of the fruity old fashion ones that only somebody who grew up with their nose in a book would know. But other parts stuck with me. Especially the part about black iron bells with rusty throats and those ghouls up there pushing them back and forth and their king yelling and dancing, enjoying the whole thing, just having a hell of a good time looking down on people below and knowing the bells were rolling a stone over their hearts.

That is what the poem said. The bells were rolling a stone over people's hearts.

That night I dreamed about the iron bells. I was down below. On a street. The king of the ghouls, he was up above in the steeple of a white church. He had a big old iron crown. He was about twice as big as a person but all out of shape. One arm bigger than the other. Big bumps all over him. I could not see his face. But I was not complaining about that. And the king was using a whip to make these other ghouls push the bells back and forth. The bells had voices. They moaned and groaned and sobbed just like the poem said they did. It was like they was not really bells at all, but living things that had been forced into that shape. And though I could not see the rest of the king's face, I could see his smile for some reason. He was flashing it right at me. This toothy white smile that seemed like it was a lot too big even for that face and he was pointing at me with a long crooked claw cause he could see straight into me and he knew the bells were rolling a stone over my heart.

I tried to run away. But my legs would not work. I tried to cover my ears. But my hands would not work. I had to just stand there, looking up while he looked down and the bells rolled a stone over my heart. Typical dream shit. Right? Wrong. Somehow this was worse. A lot worse. Like the dream had dug into some soft rotten spot deep inside of me and was twisting and turning around in there. Like somebody was poking at that rotten place with a knife and I did not have no pain killer. I woke up in a cold sweat. Glad to be in that junk pile my foster family called a spare room. That was the first time I was glad of that. Those bastards never did want me. They just wanted the monthly check for taking care of me.

I had the same dream the next night. And the next. It kept on coming.

At first, I guess I tried to pretend it was not happening. Maybe I hoped it would go away on its own. But those bells stayed stuck in my dreams. Stuck real good. I went around all day thinking about them. Worrying about them. All worn out cause I got no rest the night before and cause I was worried about what was going to happen the next night. They made a real mess of my life in just a few days. My life was not such great shakes to begin with, right? I mean growing up in and out of group homes and halfway houses and jails. Lawyers and social workers and so on will tell you there are not't any jails for kids. But they're wrong. I was practically born in a jail.

I thought about asking somebody for help. But who? And what would I say, that a dream had me on the run? Or that something was stuck up here, in my head? I did not't want everybody to start thinking I was a whack job and looking at me that way they do when they know somebody's nuts. And I sure as hell did not't want no psychiatrist of whatever poking around in my head, telling me what was wrong with me, putting me in a straight jacket, cutting off pieces of my brain.

I looked at that poem again and again in that book we had for school. I did not like looking at it but I figured maybe there was some kind of answer there. Some information that would help me fight those bells. But there was no answer. No answer at all. Just words and bells.

Then as suddenly as they started, the bells stopped.

Then it was like the last day of school, the last day of a job and the last day of one of those shitty summer programs for at risk youth all rolled into one. Holiday time. Vacation. A nonstop party. I was back in form and I made the most of it, celebrating like there was no tomorrow.

And believe me, once the bells was gone I did my best to forget them. I forced them out of my memory. And that seemed to work for a good long time. Years, in fact.

Until a few months ago, when they started up again.

I have no explanation. There are no explanations. It started out like an ordinary day. I was walking down the street to the neighborhood liquor store. I was between jobs and it was afternoon and I decided I needed a little break from all the stress about wondering where the next paycheck was going to come from and how long my uncle Bobby was going to keep letting me flop at his place. He is kind of an asshole. I was going to buy me a six pack and relax a little. I was in a pretty good mood.

I turned a corner. The same corner I had been turning for years without a problem. Then I heard the bells. Soft. Quiet. At first I told myself it was bells from some church in another part of town. But deep down I knew what it was right away. Cause there is nothing else like that sound. If you ever heard it, you would know what I mean. By the time I got to the store I was all sweaty and trembling. I knew the ghouls was up there ringing the bells and their king was looking down and laughing and pointing at me.

Pretty soon the bells was going full blast and it was just like the first time years ago. Except now was worse cause it was not just in my dreams at night. It was in the daytime when I was awake. And this time the bells did not stop. They kept going 24/7.

Some bad things in life you get used to. You build up a tolerance. Like to germs or poison or pain. For instance, you get used to people lying and cheating and shitting on you. You come to expect it. You do not even notice it no more. You get tougher. You build up scar tissue. You learn to adapt. My Uncle Bobby tells me the same thing holds true for hard work. He says you get used to it. How would he know? He has not done a hard day's work in his life unless you count sitting on his ass as a security guard eating crackers and peanut butter and watching Family Ties reruns. But that is what he says. Well, these bells are not like that. The longer they go on, the worse they get. Partly because nobody else hears them. That makes a person feel cut off, singled out in a really bad way. Like somebody really has it in for you. Then I wonder why I got stuck with this? How can some sucker who is no better than me go strolling down the street with a big smile on his stupid face without hearing these bells? Sometimes I want to split my head open and let the sounds come pouring out and drown the whole world so everyone will know what it feels like. If things worked that way, I would do it too. Believe me. I would do it in a heart beat. Share the wealth. But that is not the way things work. Life is not that fair.

I tried drinking them away. Drugging them away. Whoring them away. No use. Besides that shit costs money I don't have. I tried praying them away cause at least that is free. You can guess how much good that did. And this time I did reach out. I went to the doctor down at the clinic and he hooked me up with some other doctors and they hooked me up with some other doctors. Specialists. By now I have been prodded and poked and had all kinds of tests but they do not have the slightest idea what is causing it.

A ringing in the ears. I also hate it when the doctors call it that. It sounds too damn cute. Too sweet. Like that soft stuff about wedding bells at the beginning of that damn poem. Like jingle bells or ringing in the New Year or some crap I heard in a movie once about angels getting their wings every time a bell rings. Piss on the angels. Piss on them and their wings.

One day I finally decided to take matters in my own hands. First I drank a bottle of Cutty Sark. Then I went out to my cousin's garage where he keeps his tools and stuff. I found a screwdriver and I drove that bastard into my right ear. It hurt like a mother fucker even with all that booze in me. It was the second ear that was really hard though. That is the one that took some real courage. Cause the first one told me how much it would hurt. Understand? But I did it anyway. I drove it in real good. I figured it was worth it to get rid of those damn bells. I called 911 cause I was bleeding real bad. They brought me here and sewed me back together.

When I woke up there was all these people standing around me. Doctors and nurses. Psychiatrists probably. They were all talking but I could not hear a damn word they said. Finally a nurse held up some paper for me to read. It asked how I felt. I gave her the thumbs down. She held up another paper. It asked me how the pain was on a scale of 1 to 10. There was a big smiling face under the 1. There was a picture of a guy crying under 10. I pointed way past the 10 and laughed. She smiled but the smile looked kind of shaky. Maybe that was because she could not figure out why I was laughing. I could not stop laughing. I went on and on. I realized that although I could not hear nothing else, I could still hear the bells. It was going to be just them and me from then on. Stuck together. All alone. No other sounds. No distractions. The nurse gave me a shot of something and I fell asleep. But even then I could not get away from those big black iron bells. Ding Dong, man. Ding Dong. Shit.

By now I am ready for something really desperate. I figure I got nothing to lose. Nothing important. It has got to the point where I sometimes feel there is nothing real in my life except the bells. Like all the other things I ever heard was just made up. Like my mom singing a lullaby or some music I can really get into or a girl I like saying my name all soft and sweet. All that stuff just made up. A dream or something. I am trapped in here with just those bells ringing all the time and that king standing up there way up high looking through me and laughing and pointing and that stone rolling over my heart.

It did not take me long to decide to do the job right next time. I got something sharp from a tray in the hallway. A scalpel or something. I hid it under my clothes in the table next to me.

I decided the first chance I got when I was alone, I was going to drive that mother fucker into my head. And I was not going to stop at the ear. I was going to drive it all the way in and get rid of those bells once and for all.

Now the time has come. Nobody is around to see. I am sitting here holding the knife. It is not the idea of pain that stops me. I did it before. Twice. I can take the pain. Something else is stopping me. A question. What will happen if I drive the knife in and I drop dead and the bells still do not stop? What if I go on forever and ever hearing them?

I think I would rather wait to find out. Being stuck here with the bells is bad enough. I do not want to find out how long I might have to go on listening to them. I would rather keep some hope alive.

I throw my head back and laugh again. Of course I cannot hear the laughter. All I hear is those big black bells. Them and their damn tintinnabulation.

KYLE HEGER, former managing editor of "Communication World" magazine, lives in Albany, CA, with his wife and three sons. His writing has appeared in "The Binnacle," "eFiction," "Foliate Oak," "Milk Sugar," "Miller's Pond," "Nerve Cowboy," "Poem," "The Santa Clara Review," "Third Wednesday," "The Thorny Locust" and other publication

the scarcity of ripe peaches
Carl Miller Daniels

the sexy naked big-dicked teenage boy
notices the shape
of the lamp shade
on the lamp
on his desk,
cylindrical,
but not perfectly so. in fact,
the lamp shade is kind of deformed.
he doesn't like that. in fact,
he gets pissed off,
senses depression about to
settle in, quietly,
primly, like
it's been
invited to fill in a
hole in the back
of his head.
who'd come to his funeral,
he wonders, as
he makes the wise decision
to chop off all his
pubic hair,
lands in curly tufts
on his feet, now his
discarded pubes look like
little furry critters,
ticklish on the tops of his
monster-thin
toes.

wahoo!
Carl Miller Daniels

when i was a teenager,
i used to disappear into the woods near our house,
take off all my clothes, and jerk off,
repeatedly, sometimes 3 or 4 times
in a single afternoon. i remember
i'm spurting what felt like
two gallons of cum, all hot and gooey
and runny, and i'm all hot and sweaty and
good-looking, and my dick is hard nearly
all the time, and i'm kind of in a state
of orgiastic madness.
**

back then, i was also a
manic depressive suicidal mess.
soon to be institutionalized.
**

but, for those few hours there young and
naked and jerking off in the woods,
everything was nice,
the world was good,
and life didn't seem
nearly so crazy.

do you say "supper" or "dinner"?
Carl Miller Daniels

magritte the wallpaper and turn out the lights.
confess your sins to anyone who will listen.
promise to be good every single minute of every single day.
if you've been doing something bad, swear that you'll
stop it at once, and swear that you'll never ever do it again.
stick to your diet. watch your alcohol intake.
watch dirty movies only if they have
some meaningful artistic statement to make.
just get yourself together!
**

while walking down the road to complete and
total recovery,
the sexy naked big-dicked young man
told himself that he needed to stop
all sorts of things that he'd been doing.
too much drinking. too much
masturbating. too much
cynicism. too much criticizing
everything and everyone. he
needed to develop a sweeter nature.
a kinder attitude.
a more forgiving stance in the world.
soon the sexy naked big-dicked young man
sat down on a big smooth rock in
the middle of the woods and
thought about all these things
while he was jerking off,
thought about all these things
as he was tugging gently and rhythmically
on his big sturdy dick,
even thought about all these
things during the all-too-brief moments when
the cum was spurting out of him.
then,
the sexy naked big-dicked young man
pulled the bottle of whiskey out

of his knapsack and he sat there,
on the rock, in the middle of
the forest,
drinking whiskey and smelling
the musky scent of his
own fresh cum.
really, the world at
this moment was
all too beautiful.
how could he ever
have an
unpleasant thought
about it, or
himself, ever
ever again?
in fact, at this moment,
a bright
orange butterfly
landed on his
left nipple, and
the touch of
its delicate
and brittle little legs
made the
sexy naked big-dicked young man
grin like an
idiot, a sweet and harmless one,
with a heart
of the finest and
purest gold.

oligocene chastity
Carl Miller Daniels

while wiling away the hours,
the sexy naked big-dicked teenage boy
likes to tug on his big hard sturdy dick,
and spurt big sloppy gobs of hot gooey cum.
**

also, he runs many miles alone in
the bright sunny forest.
he gets stronger and sexier
and even better looking.
**

also, he likes shrimp puffs.
**

now you take yer average
shrimp puff
and savor it with
the tip of your tongue.
yer teeth crunching
on it till
there's next to nothing
there -- a bit of
wet dust in your
mouth -- and
that's all.
**

doesn't seem like
the average
sexy naked big-dicked teenage boy
would be "into"
shrimp puffs.
**

but he is.
**

life's kinda like that.
**

unexpected, barely
semi-logical.

**

you wish everything made
more sense than it actually
does.
**

but there he sits.
eating shrimp puffs.
**

and it's not even noon.

CARL MILLER DANIELS lives in the United States. He's not a cowboy, but thinks about them a lot. His poems have appeared in many nice places, including *Assaracus*, *BareBack Magazine*, *Chiron Review*, *Citizens for Decent Literature*, *The Commonline Journal*, *DNA Magazine*, *FUCK!*, *My Favorite Bullet*, *Thieves Jargon*, and *Zygote in my Coffee*. His book *Saline* was recently published by Interior Noise Press, and, even more recently, his chapbook *Be Kind to Strangers* was published by BareBackPress. Both books are available at Amazon. Daniels and his partner, Jon (aka "the sweetest man in the world"), have lived together for over 30 years. Check him out at http://carlmillerdaniels.tumblr.com/

Mad
Brenton Booth

I could hear some yelling and I noticed
everybody crossing to the other side of
the street. I just kept on walking. A man
screaming as loud as he could, then came
into view just ahead of me. He had on
dirty clothes—-most likely salvaged from
a garbage bin--and no shoes. He was about
six feet tall, with dirty long black hair and
an angry look on his face. He noticed me
and yelled at me, " You want some do you?
Come here dog! I'll show you what cowards
get! You are a coward! You're all cowards!
You just want to fuck up other peoples
lives." I clenched my jaw and cracked my
knuckles. I looked straight at him and
grinned. I was now ready to go. One more
word, and I'd give it to him. He looked at
me and very quickly turned and resumed yelling
at the people on the other side of the street.
Soon after walking off in silence in the
opposite direction. I shook my head as he walked
away. What a fool! I've seen as much heartache,
violence, depression, bad hangovers and
disappointment in my time as anyone. And I'm
still here, slightly. He's running away.
Convinced that it's the fault of others. Which
isn't so bad. He's just a bit unlucky really.
Today he met someone madder, than him.

Behind The Closed Door
Brenton Booth

The problem is the stars are average
and overpaid
the honest persons job is underpaid
the walls are never thick enough to
get away from the noise
the problem is the beautiful women
are ugly
the ugly women are beautiful
the men aren't strong enough for
ugly women
the problem is the cameras are
everywhere
the groceries cost too much
the car won't take us far enough
away
the problem is the gods are long
dead
the faithful have nothing else but
to continue worshipping them
our true history and future are
unknown
the problem is the great composers
are all gone
the televisions play too much
the individual has been killed by
the censorship of the masses
the problem is the sun doesn't
always shine
the relationships rarely work
the journalists use their words
to control us
the problem is the hookers charge
too much
the beautiful music never lasts
as long as it should
the oasis is always in the distance

the problem is the taxes aren't
returned
the success doesn't make you smile
victory is an idiots dream
on a Tuesday night in Sydney
all the lights off:
well almost.

BRENTON BOOTH lives in Sydney, Australia. Poetry and fiction of his has appeared in lots of small press publications. To read more of his work visit brentonbooth.weebly.com

A Man of the Cloth
Steve Slavin

If you ever saw Barbara Sackowitz walking down the street, you probably wouldn't look twice. The girl was no Marilyn Monroe, if you get my drift. We've been friends almost five years, so I'm just being objective.

Barbara and I would get together maybe once a month and have a regular girl's night out. So one night, completely out of the blue, Barbara asks me if I ever answered any of those personal ads.

"Are you kidding?" I said. "Those ads are strictly for losers. Every guy is in his fifties and wants to meet twenty-year-old chicks. Forget it! I've got plenty of better things to do with my time."

"Judy, I just asked you a simple question. You don't have to get so defensive."

"OK already. By the way, since we're on the subject, what about you?"

"*Me*? I answered just one, and that was back when I was married."

"Barbara, am I missing something here? You answered a personal ad when you were married?"

"Yeah, it was right after Robert announced to me that he was gay. And that his lover would be coming up from Baltimore to spend the weekend with us."

"Unbelievable! You did say something about that a couple of years ago, but I thought maybe he was, you know, a little effeminate. But not technically gay."

"Believe it, Judy. Robert was a certifiable fag. And get this: He said to me that he wanted to share our bed with his lover, so could I sleep in the living room?"

"What did you do?"

"I bought a copy of "The New York Review of Books" and found an ad from a guy who actually lived in Baltimore."

"A straight guy from Baltimore?"

"You better believe it. He must of thought I was nuts. I asked him two or three times, 'Are you sure that you're straight?'"

"So did you get together with him, Barbara?"

"I made a date with him for that coming weekend. In fact I took the Metroliner to Baltimore."

"You're kidding."

"No, Judy, I'm perfectly serious."

"Really? You went all the way to Baltimore on a blind date?"

"Look, there was no way I was going to be in our apartment with those two fags. I knew the marriage was over, so somehow this date made a lot of sense. In fact that's why I picked this guy— because he actually lived in Baltimore. I guess part of the appeal was that it was somehow symmetrical."

"So what happened when you got there?"

"I got off the train with all these commuters. It took a couple of minutes for the station to clear. Then there was just me standing there and there was this priest. So I figured I was stood up."

"That's pretty shabby. The guy makes you come all the way to Baltimore and then he doesn't show."

"I know. I felt like complete shit. I'm just standing there with my suitcase and the priest said to me, 'Are you Barbara?'"

"The guy was a *priest*?"

"That's what I thought! 'You're the guy who wrote the ad in "The New York Review of Books" and you're a *priest*?'"

"What did he say?"

"He said, 'No, I'm not a *priest*. I just *dressed* like a priest in case I didn't like you.'"

"Well, Barbara, at least he liked you."

"Yeah, well I was so disgusted, I was ready to get right back on the train. Also, he looked a lot older than he said he was. 'I thought you said you were 35,' I said."

"So, I lied a little."

"A little? Exactly how old are you?"

"Forty-nine."

"Barbara, what did you do?"

"I was so mad at my husband, I decided I'd give this jerk a chance. So I told him I was starving."

"Did he take you to a nice place to eat?"

"He took me to a supermarket."

"A supermarket?"

"That's right. He said he was on a tight budget. I mean, how much money do priests make? So I picked out a couple of steaks. And when we got up to the checkout, he sticks the steaks under his shirt and just walks out of the supermarket."

"What did you do?"

"I walked out after him. I guess the kid at the cash register must of been a Catholic and it didn't compute that a priest could steal."

"So then what? You went up to his place?"

"That's right. Do you want to take a guess what kind of place he lived in?"

"I'll bet it was a hovel."

"A hovel? That's too kind. He had a furnished room with a hotplate on the floor. And his bed! The sheets were gray and had stains on them."

"So what did you do?"

"Well, I figured, let me make the best of a terrible situation. I could always grab a hotel room if I had to. Anyway, I was famished, so I guess I was lucky that I like my steak rare."

"Did you eat on the floor?"

"Actually, he had one chair, which he gallantly offered to me. Then, when we were about half way finished eating, he yells, 'Let's fuck!'"

"You *didn't!*"

"How could I resist that approach?"

"So what did you do?"

"Judy, if we had been in New York, I would have just walked out of there. But then I thought about those two fairies have sex in *my* bed.

"Well, I gritted my teeth, took off my clothes, and lay down on those disgusting sheets. and thought to myself -- how bad can it possibly be?"

"So you did it with the priest?"

"Yes."

"So how was it?"

"Best lay I ever had."

A recovering economics professor, Steve Slavin earns a living writing math and economics books. *This story first appeared in *Horror, Sleaze, Trash* on October 27, 2015.

Books
Michael Estabrook

How many books
have I read in my lifetime you wonder
one per week my entire
adult life
that's 2,444 books give or take
and for what?

To get into college?
already done that

To get a good job?
they don't care if you've read 24,440 books

To get into heaven?
there isn't one
and I've never heard
of people reading up there anyway

To win the prettiest girl?
already done that
she's here next to me sleeping soundly
while I'm reading yet another stupid book.

My Girl
Michael Estabrook

She likes her cereal soggy
can't swallow pills
makes the bed as she's crawling out of it
takes baths not showers
doesn't drink or swear
can't go to bed without emptying the dishwasher
is always on a diet but refuses to call it a diet
moves her lips while she's reading
always changes our table in restaurants
never sweats
loves puzzles, giraffes, and mangoes
doesn't keep any houseplants
doesn't like eating fish or swimming in the ocean
amazing what you learn about a woman
after being with her 45 years.

MICHAEL ESTABROOK is a recently retired baby boomer child-of-the-sixties poet freed finally after working 40 years for "The Man" and sometimes "The Woman." No more useless meetings under florescent lights in stuffy windowless rooms. Now he's able to devote serious time to making better poems when he's not, of course, trying to satisfy his wife's legendary Honey-Do List.

Bush Era Tattoos
Steven Storrie

I got these tattoos when
George W. Bush was President
When there was a war on something called
Terror
The Patriot Act, WMD's and Guantanamo
And nobody knew what the fuck was going on

The leader of the free world
Didn't care about black people
A singer said
And was secretly glad to see them getting washed away
His brother liked to hang with a guy named Chad
In Florida or something
And together they pulled off the greatest robbery
The country had ever seen

Hadn't he been an alcoholic in his youth?
A waste of skin and space?
Someone best thrown onto a Nascar track
At the Indy 500
And left to fend for himself?
A man who, when faced with the prospect of war
In some place they called 'Nam
had ran to his over indulgent Daddy
Who told him with experienced conviction
Don't worry, son
Money will get you out of this.

I my mind I see him in a classroom
Reading to kids all seated beneath him
Kids who probably read at a higher level
Than he did
All wondering who the fuck this old guy was
Who couldn't get his mouth around
6th grade words.
Who held the book like it was a foreign object

And kept stammering like he was caught in a lie
I see the aide lean in and tell him the news
The news that changed everything
Changed the world
the news coming out of New York City
something about two planes and the World Trade Centre
he sits
and he sits
and he sits
a glazed look on his face
wondering if Spot the dog
is ever gonna catch that ball
before someone in the Secret Service
says to him in a whisper
Mr President
Don't you think we'd better go?

I can still see him standing at Ground Zero
Stood atop the rubble
Of concrete and steel
Revelling in feeling like
One of the boys]
One of the regular joe's
Who'd buy him a beer
If he ever wandered into their bar
On the corner of some cold street
In the middle of downtown Pittsburgh
He's crowing into a megaphone
Arm draped around someone
Hired from the lines
Of a Bruce Springsteen song
In order to denote authenticity
And how he's one of us
His bemused look has faded
Now he's enjoying himself
He thinks it's a deleted scene
From a new Bruce Willis movie
As his head cranks up
He's playing to the crowd
He hears us, he says

The rest of the world
Can hear us too
And the people who knocked these buildings down
Will hear all of us soon.

Somewhere in a room that wreaks of leather furniture
And the vilest abuses of power
Dick Cheney is laughing his ass off
Slugging 100 year old whiskey
And abusing the Thai houseboy

I got these tattoos
When George W. Bush was President.

When Anna Kournikova Was My Next Door Neighbour
Steven Storrie

I sat dick in hand
waiting for the screen to fully download
This was in the days of dial up internet
Days when everything was slower
Better days, some say
Some, but not me
I used to see her sometimes
but she never talked to me
So I sat in my room
Sweating in the heat of summer '97
Waiting to see up her skirt
The picture is taking it's time
Creeping lower inch by inch
Then someone calls the house phone
and my connection drops right out
I'm left with just a blonde ponytail
beneath a white tennis cap
and broad, bronzed shoulders for sport
Some kind of half-baked monster
Not quite finished not quite whole
Still, I do it anyway
She couldn't play tennis for shit
And I realise right there and then
Both our lives are already falling apart.

STEVEN STORRIE has worked as a cable T.V repair man, dishwasher, choreographer, ice cream vendor and junk yard attendant. He is currently locked in his basement working on his first collection of poetry, bickering with his neighbours and storing the baseballs he keeps when they are hit into his yard. You can find him at @renegadepriest1

Resurrection Man
Cyn Bermudez

Chief wore only black, a by-product from his Goth days: skinny jeans, black Durango boots, and a Black Metal t-shirt. He fringed the ends himself. Each strand exactly one-inch in length. A technique he had perfected during the summer he moved from the armpit of America to its navel. A new home, new foster parents, and no friends—he had plenty of time to perfect his look. With the exception of the fringe, he didn't grunge his clothes or wear black eyeliner anymore or that god awful black nail polish given to him by his ex, Gertie—the girl from the East Side, his little Mexican doll, who wore just as much eyeliner as he did. Chief washed his hair every day now, too. And he always wore the silver cross good luck charm he had bought from a blonde-haired woman who called herself Moonstone because she was one-sixteenth Chumash. It hung on his neck long and heavy, like the wooden rosary Gertie had placed around her rear view mirror.

He held the cross between his fingertips as he waited for Li outside the city morgue. Doc hid in the van. Chief's lanky frame silhouetted a curved monstrosity drawn by the flickering streetlight against the yellowed air, the poor posture Gertie had hated. He slouched almost defiantly now in protest. His foot tapped, rapid, like a savage drum in the midst of cannibals. He waited for Li to wheel out their next corpse. White smoke billowed out of him.

Glass shattered, breaking the silent night. The clanking shards muffled by wood and plaster until the door jangled open. A metal gurney caught midway through the entrance, its wheel stuck behind the door jam. The hole-splattered white sheet Chief brought from home tugged slightly. Short hair egressed at Chief's end: scruffy, each follicle dry and rough, like horsehair on a cheap wig. He knew not even the hair would be left once the cutters got their hands on the body. The hair would soon be donned on a balding head.

After his first run to the cutters, he had bought Gertie a pendant, the patron saint of their city: Saint Barbara. She smiled wide, her eyes sparkling. Gertie kissed him long, biting softly on his lower lip, and then resumed her inquiry. She had asked him about the body parts: Where did they go? He didn't know, didn't care. And then she had asked: Well, aren't you curious? Not really. But he actually *had* thought about the bodies: pieces of mulcted flesh to quiet Death.

The five hundred dollar economy plan gave some family a wooden box and their loved one parted out. Those were the quick jobs. On a good night, and tonight was a good night, they'd scored a John Doe—some poor sap with no family, no one to care about his afterlife. He and the gang, Chief mused, like Robin and his coterie, except they stole from the dead.

Gertie had protested the means, not the end. It's not right, she had said once. And Chief said, well Doc was family. And she said, no, a foster parent, especially a former one, wasn't *real* family. But Doc had always been there for him, the first to take him in as a newborn.

"Secure the damned thing better this time." Doc leaned his big head outside the van window, a cigarette dangled from his lips. "No sliding around in the back like last time." At the back of the van, doors spread eagle, Chief and Li tightened the rope in perfect Boy Scout knots. Doc never lifted a damn finger.

Doc and Li were stuck with Chief like two bears thrown together, tail-tips attached to him. They were the coffin and mourners, two sons who sought vengeance for their fates. Li, who never let anyone meet his parents, only spoke Mandarin in whispers. And Doc, who had twenty years on them, used to be a cutter of a different kind, sculpted people and made them beautiful.

"Stop worrying about the stiff, Old Man. I got this." Li tapped the side of the van and Doc drove away. The motor hummed, serenading the night, until a bump later: The cadaver skidded across, bouncing with each thud in the road. Doc swerved, his head craning back. The cigarette fell from his lips, and he bounced and patted the burning cigarette in his lap.

No one wanted to look at the dead man, especially Chief. He accidentally glimpsed part of the corpse's hand and body—porcelain skin, jagged black line cracking under tattered army fatigues. His yellow stained thermals smelled of piss and alcohol.

The first dead body Chief had ever seen was Mrs. Buckley in the third grade: Her black wig—wiry and thick—fell off-centered from her face. She collapsed during fractions. Her hand landed by his feet. In her casket, she had cooled to a waxy finish, her cheek ice-cold on his lips, a polite kiss forced on him by his temporary foster mother. He had nightmares for weeks; he slept on the floor in his foster mom's room as he held onto a rosary and recited half-prayers and hail-Mary's.

Chief shivered with the cold as the van zigzagged down the street. Colorful language flung through the air. Doc blamed Li and Li blamed Chief. Crisscross words flung threw the air as the body slid out, rolling on the ground, a life-sized plastic doll. Doc didn't stop until the van rolled up onto a curb. They watched from their motorized cave the people passing by the John Doe. No one ever looked at the man.

When Gertie's auntie had died, Chief promised a clean sale: A five hundred dollar economy plan—for real this time—no cutters for his girl. He had spoken to Doc himself. She's your girlfriend's sister, he had said. And Doc rolled his eyes and said whatever, dude. But good hair and strong bones ran in the family and Doc couldn't resist the extra grand. Chief wondered if Gertie suspected. There was a look in her eyes whenever she had asked about his conversation with Doc. She'd make him repeat, step by step: "What did you say," and then "what did he say?" Doc never admitted to Chief about the empty box under the ground but Chief knew. And he knew no one would look or ask or even care about the Poor Man's Burial package.

When the street cleared, Chief and Li went to the John Doe, clothes now stripped by the indigenous street creatures. They lugged his body, feet dragged and heavy, back to the van. Chief looked away, pointedly, and Li laughed.

"You act like this is some *Thriller* shit," Li said. He tossed the white sheet to him. "Cover his face if you need to." The sheet landed by the dead man's face. Chief couldn't move, not even if he wanted to.

Doc peeled out yelling back at Chief and Li to cover and secure the cadaver. Chief blind-patted his hand toward the sheet, his knees locked. He heard Li laugh again. So Chief opened his eyes, feeling like a kid again, taunted by classmates into do something he knew was stupid. He looked down at the face: rounded eyes, dark, with matching raven hair. He fell backward. His own face stared up at him. Except the face was sun burnt and leathery, like it saw too many nights without shelter. Li looked at Chief and then looked at the dead man's face, too. He jumped back and hit his head. Doc stopped the van to see what the hell was going on.

"Pod people," Li said and looked at Chief. Doc rolled his eyes and covered the body quickly.

"You alright, man," Doc said. Chief said nothing.

Li poked at Chief, asking him about their past, things only the two of them knew. He would recount part of a story and pause and wait for Chief to fill in the rest. He didn't. He couldn't speak, and Li's voice sounded like a distant saxophone.

In the quiet of his mind, woodwind and brass trumped as the van walls gave way to the day before: Gertie had cried a lot, an ultimatum had been made. No more golden corpses she demanded. Chief couldn't do the straight and narrow, not even for the new life they had created. Her voice became a distant wind as she hurled her heartache at him. He had sat there stoically on the sofa as he did now in the van.

Li prodded him. The world swirled around him. Li and Doc and Gertie, bodies of mass and compressed light, delicate balances of outward pressure and gravity imploding and exploding at the same. His reality, a supernova event, a star collapsed in on itself, where nothing was left but traces of his life that couldn't escape the deadly radius of circumstance.

"Will you quit," Doc said to Li. "He's not a damn pod person, you idiot." Doc had driven up to an area just outside the city, a desolate place where people lived in cardboard huts and heated themselves by trashcan fires.

"Where are we at?" Li asked as they both got out of the van. Doc pulled out a couple of shovels and tossed one to Li. "What is this for? We have to meet the cutters."

Doc gave Li a look and then nodded in Chief's direction. Li looked at Chief and then back at Doc. He nodded his head in surrender. Under the new moon, while flame and embers flickered into the air, Doc and Li buried the dead man.

CYN BERMUDEZ came into this world in love with the night sky. Obsessed with stars and galaxies and the eternal existential crisis of why we are here, she went on to study physics at the University of California, Santa Barbara. After completing her degree in physics, she found her home in fictional worlds, where she can explore the what-ifs of the universe. For more about Cyn, please visit her website at cynbermudez.com

Brad
Wayne F. Burke

I worked as house painter
for Brad
who weighed 300 pounds
and was afraid to go
up the ladders;
I painted the world white
all summer
and got blasted on pot
with Brad, a stoner
who bought a 16 oz. hot chocolate
and a hot dog every morning
before lighting the first joint;
he told me that
he watched porno films
sometimes and
asked what I thought of
him doing that?
(not much)
He told me that his wife
took it up the ass
but only when she was drunk.
He could be a prick at work
sometimes but
was a decent sort
though lost.

Boston Cream
Wayne F. Burke

Sometimes I go to Dunkin' Donuts
for coffee
and while in line
think about the doughnuts
maybe even consider a crueler
or plain stick
sometimes fantasize about
a Boston Cream
which
I would never order
because of my diabetes
or a chocolate glazed
either
it's the same as
thinking about Miss America
in my bed
with her legs spread
a far-out fantasy
that cannot be sustained
but
what about a reduced fat muffin,
it is a possibility,
one less remote
than
the beauty queen.

Vane
Wayne F. Burke

Mr. Gootay, from India
owned a funky restaurant
on the backside of Harvard Square
in Cambridge, Massachusetts
where I worked as fry cook
putting out breakfasts
and lunches
and sweating my hangovers
off
over a sizzling grill
that baked my brain
and made me thirsty again,
and one night after work,
in a bar
in Central Square
where Harvard does not live,
I got the shit beat out of me,
and the next morning
I went to work wearing
mirror sunglasses and
band-aids on my face,
and Mr. Gootay asked
"what happened, Vane?"
and I said "I walked into a door,"
and Mr. Gootay,
standing with hands behind his back
and wearing a short white jacket
that made him look like a doctor,
said "unbeLEAVEable!"

Trailways
Wayne F. Burke

I stood outside the bus station
one night in
Burlington, Vermont
after hitting the bars
which I'd got thrown out of
one after the other
and I puked a geyser
of mustard-colored whatever
that splashed the sidewalk
and my shoe tops
and a bus driver with a stricken
look
asked "did you do that?"
and I said "no'
and he told me he should not
allow me on the bus
but I plowed up the stairs
and got on
and sat in back
where I added
to the stench
until I got off
an hour later
in the state capital of
Montpeculiar.

WAYNE F. BURKE was born in Adams, Massachusetts and raised by his paternal grandparents. He attended the University of Massachusetts—where he was a member of the freshman football team—and three other institutions of higher learning before graduating from Goddard College in 1979. His stories, essays, reviews, and poems have appeared in numerous publications. He has two other collections of poetry, published by BareBackPress: *Words that Burn* (2013), *Dickhead* (2015), and *Knuckle Sandwiches* (2016).

Happy Secretary's Day
Brenda Kern

A man is supposed to open the car door for a woman on a date—everybody knows this. And I don't think he did. Our first date, and he didn't open the door for me, unless the trunk counts as a door.

My cell phone is ringing again—for the fourth time now. I can't answer it. I can't move, so I can't even turn it off. Eventually it won't have any charge left, anyway. I'm sure that's the ever-faithful roommate calling. She said not to go. She said I had only met him yesterday; his name might not even be Rex ...um, Fletcher? Fuller? Something like that. Anyway—she said if I wasn't home by midnight she would call. It must be well past midnight by now.

He came into the shop to look for a card for his secretary, he said. I directed him to the section on cards for Secretary's Day, and he found one—it showed a jukebox on the cover with musical notes coming out of it, and the inside said, "You keep this office rockin'!" Lame. But, he flirted with me. I'm no beauty queen, and edging on spinster territory, so this was banner news. And he asked me out! He said he'd pick me up today at 6 o'clock.

Only six hours ago! (Or seven?) I wasn't bloody then, but I was very ...giddy, almost girlish.

Things were going well, I thought. We went to a little diner—not fancy, but clean. He seemed at the time to be the strong, silent type.

He certainly is strong. That's why it only took the one blow to paralyze me like this. He thinks I'm dead.

If only I hadn't been so safety-conscious! I had trouble fastening my seat belt when we left the diner, and said that there was something stuck in the buckle. I fished around in the mechanism with my nail file and got it—a slim gold band. I said "Look—a wedding ring!"

This was a mistake on my part, and the date went poorly after that.

He said nothing, but I could see the muscles in his jaw working as he floored it. We sped through town until we got to the old steel mill, closed for years.

He asked if I would like to see his office, got out of the car first, and came around to my side. I'm sure now—he didn't open the door, I did. I turned my back to him to close it, and that's when he hit me.

And put me in the trunk.

There's someone else here. Or some of her—I glimpsed something just before he tossed me in and shut the trunk, and I've just figured out what I saw. It's hard to recognize a shape as a human body without the head.

I wonder if they make a greeting card that says, "Sorry you were buried alive on your first date."

BRENDA KERN lives in beautiful Colorado, and she enjoys writing articles and essays on a variety of subjects, short fiction, and sometimes even poetry.

unethical advertising practices and the apathetic consumer
Ben Newell

The salesgirl at the store
looks nothing like
the salesgirl in the commercial;
she is the flat hamburger,
the one which looked
so flavorful and juicy
on TV. She is the backpage hooker
peering at you behind
a security chain, hardly
the young lady in
the posted pic—
This con will endure;
we have grown accustomed
to the trick, expecting
mediocrity and/or
downright inferiority.
We feel unworthy
of anything better.
We are too weary
to protest, taking it
without a peep
of dissent,
perpetuating the
chicanery,
buying the shoes,
feeding our face,
fucking her,
anyway.

the sports illustrated swimsuit issue
Ben Newell

Here at the college library
I place the current magazines and journals
on our display rack,
a rather pointless task
as the interest in print has waned
to almost nothing,
even our most salacious offering
is largely ignored;
I imagine Sisyphus feels this way,
rolling that big ass rock
up and down and up and—

—prior
to this gig
I worked at a large public library
where she was plucked and passed
from perv to perv,
invariably ending up on the restroom floor;
I always wore latex gloves
when handling her.

But these overachieving millennials
don't seem enticed
in the least;
I put her up several days ago
and she hasn't moved an inch,
leaving her all for me,
my very own paper concubine
to help with this
absurdity.

BEN NEWELL is a fortysomething library clerk in the Jackson, Mississippi area. His poems have appeared in BareBack, Carcinogenic Poetry, LUMMOX, Nerve Cowboy, Pink Litter, and other underground publications. His BDSM crime novella, Christy in Cuffs, was recently published by Comet Press. He hates cold weather.

crueller than kids
Matthew J. Hall

when his father died
the other boys were
exceptionally cruel

taunting him at every turn
about his dead dad

one fat-faced kid
all cheeks and lips
and a tongue too big
for his mouth
made up a song

and they sang it
in the playground

your old man's dead
your mum ate his head
your sister put the body
in the garden shed

they sang it over and over
in the cloak room
and in the corridors
and in the canteen

years later
in one of many factories
I spotted him
I saw the boy with a dead dad
only he was a man
and so was I

I switched off the
shrink-wrap machine
and walked over to

the end of the packing line

I asked him about the years
in between now and then
he told me he had been in and out
of work and in and out of hospitals
and various other institutions

he spoke with slow purpose
as though he couldn't quite trust
the words to form as he'd intended

he picked up a heavy box
and put it onto a pallet of other
identical heavy boxes

it's good here isn't it?
he said
he wasn't being sarcastic
he meant it

he told me that in hospital
he'd met a girl
who let him be her boyfriend
in fair exchange for medication

he told me this while he finished
stacking and wrapping the boxes
then he pulled the pallet with a pump-truck
into the loading bay and started all over again

I told him
I thought they'd given him
a rough time at school
I told him
kids can be so cruel

he asked if I'd kept up
with any of them
I told him, no

he continued stacking
box after box and his
sweat patches spread

I asked him if he had
kept up with any of them

he stopped working and said
no fucking way
kids can be cruel
but adults are crueller

then he went back to his work
and I went back to mine

angel
Matthew J. Hall

angel learnt her lessons early on;
life wouldn't be what it was supposed to be
and it wasn't supposed to be much of anything at all

the tasks and the chores were just that
nothing less
nothing more
the mutt's tail must be chased

pleasure and pain do not come in equal measure
they just come and then they go

so much of this is hard to swallow
like a chunk of stubborn meat in a toothless mouth

but angel learnt her lessons early on
and if the steak didn't melt on her tongue
she spat it out

tea for two
Matthew J. Hall

numb in the hell
of a dead marriage
she watched
from her side of the
breakfast table
as he removed
a tiny piece of egg shell
from the tip of
his tongue

he placed the shell
on the plate's edge
then forked another
mouthful of egg

she considered this
and concluded;
our life is a
weak cup of tea

how are your eggs?
she asked
good, he said, thank you

no bother
she said

then she went into
the kitchen
where she boiled water
and made a pot of tea
for two

another life, another world
Matthew J. Hall

one of
the factory
girls
the one with
other worlds
for eyes
used to flirt
with me
at the
production
line

but I
was young
and naïve
and my
wife to be
was
pregnant

my son
was inside
stretching her
belly
kicking
eager to scream
at the world
outside

the factory
girl
fluttered lashes
over other
worlds
but I was
young and naive

and my
wife to be was
pregnant

even as a child

she wondered about death
her father told her
stop moping about

these are the best days of
your life
stop bloody crying
or I'll give you something
to really cry about
I'm the one that ought cry
try working for a living
you'll see
you'll see what it's all about

even as a child
she thought about the days
days passed
and days to come

she watched her father
eating boiled fish
picking the bones from
two lines of teeth
and drinking endless
cups of tea
and she wondered
about death

MATTHEW J. HALL is a UK writer based in Bristol. His poetry chapbook, Pigeons and Peace Doves is available through Blood Pudding Press. He reviews small press books at www.screamingwithbrevity.com

Playmate
Edward Anki

I have a purple bruise
on my arm
where my girlfriend pinched and twisted
the last time
we played Scrabble.

We usually play Scrabble
while drinking
and on this particular occasion
I was winning
handsomely
and making jackass
remarks.

"Don't be frustrated. It's marvellous what you do
with such a tiny little brain."

"Why don't you go fuck yourself?"

"Now honey," I told her, "your language, please . . ."

She reached out,
inflicted the physical abuse,
stared intently back down
at the board.

Finding somebody
special
can be challenging.

I topped up
her wine.

Niagara Falls
Edward Anki

We got the room
with the heart-
shaped Jacuzzi
and ordered real
inauthentic Chinese
food and towards midnight
I drew back the heavy curtains
and drinking deeply
from Sauvignon Blanc
filled Styrofoam
saw it:

Time,
over
flowing.

Cleaner
Edward Anki

Early Wednesday afternoon
in a food court
in the heart of the financial district
I raise my gaze
see her clearing refuse
from a nearby table
think she's built
like a troll
the poor dear
she looks like a troll.

I notice her earrings:
dream catchers.

Worthy Stench
Edward Anki

The middle-aged barmaid
reeks of two failed
marriages

one miscarriage
seventeen one-night stands
one dead parent
one hundred and seventy-six thousand
cigarettes
one aborted acting career
twenty-one hundred
shots of tequila
four hundred thousand
sighs
and a good
heart.

I've got a nose
for
poetry.

EDWARD ANKI resides in Toronto, Canada. His poetry has previously appeared in several magazines and journals, including *Qwerty, Urban Graffiti, BareBackMagazine, Mad Poets Review*, and *The Chaffin Journal*. He has also been featured on *The Emerging Writers Reading Series, The Art Bar Poetry Series, The Blue Coffee Reading Series* and *The Boneshaker Reading Series*. His first published collection of poetry, *Remote Life*, was published in 2014 by BareBackPress.

RULES TO LIVE BY:
Lee Thorn

#1. Nobody wants
to get sucked off
by a guy with
dirty fingernails.

homecoming
Lee Thorn

I had a lucky war
ridiculously lucky

the army cut me loose in oakland
saying they owed me a thousand
dollars and would I like
it in fifties

I went to the nearest men's room
and stuffed my uniform in a tall
green trash can

someone flushed a toilet came out
of a stall and said "I know
exactly how you feel"

my cab driver was a middle-aged
stocky black guy who knew
immediately that I was a
brand new civilian and thought
he knew just what a brand new
civilian needed. "I used to
run a few girls here in town"

his offer of a whore made me
smile my first wide civilian
smile. he looked over the
seat and smiled back

"this is my first half hour of
being a civilian" he laughed
"I know exactly how you feel"
I said "I'll give you fifty bucks
to blow you"

he drove to an empty floor of a

parking garage, opened his door
and swung his feet out

I came around and kneeled on the
greasy concrete to suck his ample rod
"oh yeah baby. you need that.
sooo hungry. go baby go"

swallowing his heavy load I'm
thinking "free at least. free at
last. holy fucking jesus I'm
free at last"

an otherwise sane neighbor
calls the fire department
to remove diamondbacks
from her yard

not that they mind.
we don't have fires around here
and I'm sure they get bored
as hell just playing
grab-ass all day

a raucous young posse of
four or five responds

and my neighbor will bake
something special and take
it to the station
the next day

the guys drop the snakes
off just a little way up
the road so it won't be
too hard to find their
way home

a cambodian friend
a fellow vet
once told me that
his little village would
sometimes have a big
rice surplus and they'd
take the whole year off

and everybody would just
loaf and horse around
and drink palm beer
and go fishin' for
a whole year

but Ly was a jokester
and I could never be sure
when he was spinnin' tales

like he claimed that he
once spent 24 hours in
a whorehouse and got
his rocks off ten times

LEE THORN is an outsider writer/artist best known for his poetry/art zine *FUCK!*, which published monthly from 1998 to 2011 and was collected by several universities. He's led troops in combat, fought for gay rights, resisted anti-dope laws, taught at the university and college levels, and run a boring business. Bereft of his 30-year partner, he's retired and looking for sex in all the wrong places.

Witnesses
Michael Dennis

I feel hampered by witnesses
as I stand by and do nothing

we all hear the same laments
the church bells tell us so

we are the selfish ruin
on fresh cut grass

dark winds caress our dreams
as orange-haired zealots
ignite garbage with gasoline

I feel hampered by witnesses
and am nothing

and you are nothing too
it's not unusual

something will happen soon enough
we can be sure of it

Tombstone
Michael Dennis

I am the Doc Holiday of Canadian poetry
a drunken gunslinger angry at the world

walked into a reading last week
and shot the unsuspecting poet
right between his surprised eyes

picked the mic out of the air,
the dead poet wouldn't need it,
and rattled off my latest

the audience was luke warm at best
but I still had some bullets

and was confident
that they would all love me soon

Last at bat
Michael Dennis

I felt like Yogi Berra
"I made the wrong mistake."
it wasn't the first time

we are rarely the heroes we wish to be
our kingdoms, sad small affairs

I remembered the right thing
and then didn't do it

because I was lazy
my selfish self sucking

all the air
out of the room

next door the dog lounged on the porch
licked his own balls because he could

two doors away the mailman approached
the bright sun framing him from behind

it was time to clear the bases
so I stepped up to the plate

Winter
Michael Dennis

snow moving across ice
like a murmuration of starlings

it is a particularly Canadian beauty
for we find it so in our hearts

as much as winter is a test
we frolic like nymphs in the snow

in a few weeks spring will begin
flowers singing electric

children will return to our quiet street
and we will return to our front porch

where we will drink wine
in the evening

watch the sun go down
forget that winter ever happens

MICHAEL DENNIS has been publishing poetry for almost forty years. *Bad Engine: New and Selected Poems* (Anvil Press) will be out in the spring of 2017

DST
Ian Thomas Malone

Daylight savings, where twice a
Year, the clocks are allowed to
Move unnaturally forward. Eww.

All because a bunch of people
Sat in a room and decided that
This looked like a good idea.

How many more life hacks are
Out there, waiting to be wished
Into existence just like that?

I fear for the calendar. Fall
Could get fucked if summer
Decides it wants a little more.

What about countries? Lines
Look easier to move than time.

Soon a spoon will become a
Fork, and the moon will host
The 2017 Spring Olympics.

Which isn't to say that I'm
Completely against Daylight
Savings. I just want people
To understand that we have
Rules and if we're going to
Change them, there's a few
More I'd like to take a look at.

Projecting
Ian Thomas Malone

Hey you! Yea, you right there.
Come over here and solve all
My problems. I have candy.
Well, just a Twix from Halloween.

In exchange, you will fix everything.
That's right. Everything. All of it.

My problems are your problems
Because I want them to be.

You will stop what you are doing
And you will help me. I want you to.

That's all there is to it.

Our problem, our, as the individual,
Are ours. People can help, sometimes.

But you, yourself. You have the power.

Use it.

More
Ian Thomas Malone

Fulfillment. A problem of the bored, the
Unobligated, those with time to spare.

I didn't say the rich, for fulfillment isn't
A matter of wealth. Rather, a state of mind.

To want more is only natural, human.
Perfectly fine. That elusive "more," which
Is always out there, waiting to be chased.

Until you start to whine about more.
Then you can go and fuck yourself.

What We Have
Ian Thomas Malone

What we have is what we have.
The best book can't be one that
Was never written, even if it's
One of Homer's lost treasures.

Pistachio can't be the best flavor
Of chocolate ice cream, despite
Vanilla's desire to corner the market.

Order creates purpose, for those
Who need to believe that even
The most peculiar quirks of the
World can be put neatly into place.

What if the best reality is the dream?
To accept that would be to allow chaos
The chance to mess everything up, the
Order we work so hard to maintain.

A categorical anarchy. Good or bad?
Not for me to say, though a world
Where pistachio can be the best kind
Of chocolate ice cream doesn't sound
So bad to me, as long as it wins on merit.

IAN THOMAS MALONE is a writer. He wrote the above poems.

Need Cock
Karina Bush

Unlock my slut
With cock
No love
No need
Too complicated
Need cock
Man working hard
Man and cock
Working man smell
Cock for slut response
Dig with it
Dig her out

Come Away
Karina Bush

Come away, human man
You have a soul
I can show you
You've shown me
Human love
Your anger
Your rushes
In the quest
For holy
An angel
A fairy
I trail light
And charm
You
Fly with me
My lover
Until our heads are silver
And God shines here

Bitch
Karina Bush

A toilet-cleaning
Brown thing
You are
Ubiquitous
Bitch
I'm whole
White
Supreme
So white
So pink
Daddy's Angel
Forever
Blinding
See my ring?
Keep bleaching

Bestial
Karina Bush

Jeans and a belt
On bone and guts
Straightened erect to stand tall
Instead of moving
Close to earth
Down low
This man-animal
Big and pure and bulging
By day he will impress with words
By night he will roll and teem
For his huntress
Bringing to her
The mysteries of the wild

KARINA BUSH is an Irish poet. Her first poetry collection 'Maiden' has recently been published by 48th Street Press. For more visit *karinabush*.com.

A VALENTINE POEM FOR ALL THE MAD REDHEADS
Bradford Middleton

Blood red hair and a dose of the insane is how I like them

And the one at the minute wow, she simply takes my breath away

I'm like a sex-crime waiting to happen, scared and worried about
how I may
behave

That's a bit of a lie but hey when she's around I just want to listen,
take
notes

And gaze in to her wondrous eyes as the hand not taking notes holds
on

With all his might to his pint of some imported beer

He could so easily fall for this one, she just hits all the right buttons

A brain the size of a colossus and a body that just makes me come
over in a
cold sweat

From head to toe, whilst I sit baffled at what she is saying

She grabs the attention of the table with her deep insights

And not just on the obvious every-day things;

I didn't want to turn this in to a love poem but I always had a
weakness
for drop-dead gorgeous mad red-heads!

LUSTFUL THOUGHTS IN A RETAIL ENVIRONMENT
Bradford Middleton

At work on the check-out and I've nothing to look forward too

Not until just one of them comes through my door

As desperate for lunch as I am for chatter and flirtation

And a chance to spin my magic, chatting books and music and

To all intense and purposes acting like a human

My beady set of eyes will peer up as soon as she appears and I'll get ready

And as she joins the queue I tell my colleague no, I don't need any help

Not right now, wait for her to come and then she blows it

My eager little colleague logs in and offers her service and doesn't even
ID her

For a big bottle of rum that just looks to be shared

But not tonight as she turns for the door before her eyes catch mine

A smile prevails over her face as I see her walk past, back to work

It seems none of the women I like drink in any of the bars I drink in

So to this day I'm left alone drunk in bars with women who hate me

Or simply ignore me, casting me as a black-spot in their otherwise
beautiful existences...

But when they come in to our shop, it almost makes me want to do overtime

Their succulent bodies are ripe for the taking and ooze a sexuality of tender naivety

When they flirt back I just wish I could leap over the counter and saunter
off

Leaving the queue to become confused as I go chase my lustful concerns

She'd be everything I'd want, good music, good films, good music, the lot

A dash of dyed red would go down a storm as would a slutty attitude to
clothing

All of that and a filthy mind and boy oh boy would you be mine?

THE DESTRUCTION OF OUR PLAYGROUND
Bradford Middleton

It all feels like shit

As I again find myself

Sitting here

Wallowing once more

In reflection of past times

And how I miss them so

But the people

Well their lives have moved on

And those buildings

And streets that were

Filled with such

Potential for fun

It's all mostly gone

Soho was our diamond

In the rough, Bloomsbury's

Down-at-heel urchin

Brother with plenty

To tempt a teenage

Suburbanite. Those first nights

Wandering around, learning

The streets, the alleys

Every inch of every road

Every pub and record

And bookshop, back

Then I knew them all

Wanted a drink at 5am

No problem, I'd know

Somewhere, coffee on

A 24 hour drip feed

For when the speed was

Wearing thin and I was

Unsure of how I'd get home

But now, post CR, Soho rebranded

As a trendy, family-friendly place

Where you can go buy a Starbucks

Whenever they are open,

Kool Eddie never shut,

Some of us convinced he

Never slept. Bars now rule

And all around they all shut

At 11pm, shut up shop

Thrown into the night air

With nowhere to go as

All the clubs I used to go to

Are no longer there and

All the late bars have shut

Questionable licences may have

Finally been questioned. Now walking

Down any street is akin to entering

A disaster movie depicting

The destruction of a previously

Great city that has been

Orchestrated by those in charge

In a desperate

Every city needs a radical heart

And London has lost its

With the slow march towards

Gentrification and the end

Of our little playground.

THE GARDEN OF ENGLAND
Bradford Middleton

It was the most terrifying place

On the whole of planet earth

Or at least that's what I thought

Walking down a quiet country lane

With signs, a million signs, all telling me

It was dangerous to do this

Forbidden to do that and some things

That just made me think

Would anyone really want to do that

In the first place, fuck sake don't say

The people of Kent are as stupid as they

Often seem to be with their right-wing

Anti-migrant views and love of living

In England's so-called garden

But I was here to read some poems

Spend the night under the sky with

Nothing but a sleeping bag between

Me and the elements and once I'd read

Sleep came easily as yet again I launched

A tirade against good sense and

Drank and smoked my way to my bed

BRADFORD MIDDLETON lives in Brighton on England's south-coast having come of age in the depths of south-east London. He began writing at the age of 36 and now has over 200 unique publications by a whole host of different websites/ magazines/ small presses. His debut chapbook was published last year by Crisis Chronicles Press and his new one was recently published by Holy & Intoxicated Press. He also has a novel out through New Pulp Press entitled Dive which no one has read because they fear it will send them mad. He occasionally tweets @beatnikbraduk.

Crazy Betty
C.M. Gabbett

Why the fuck are we open until 11 on a Tuesday?

Ellen pondered that question as she scanned a stack of books lining the counter of the customer service desk. She was exhausted. This was her second shift, after a long day at the office. Student loans sucked.

As she scanned through several self-help books, she was approached by a middle-aged African-American woman. The woman wore plain brown pants and a cheetah print top. Ellen cringed.

Really? Again?

The woman approached the counter and began tapping her long, red acrylic nails on the fake wood.

Ellen did her best not to show how much she did not want to deal with this woman. She turned to her and flashed her the biggest, sweetest, most insincere smile that she could muster.

"Hi Betty!" she chirped. "How can I help you tonight?"

Betty looked up at her, a very serious expression on her face. "Do you work here?"

"Yes, I do." *Just like the last five times I've helped you in the past two weeks.* "What can I do for you?"

Betty pulled a decrepit looking journal out of her bag and proceeded to flip to the back page. She read it for a second, then asked "Do you have the July 1986 issue of Finger Paints Magazine?"

Ellen blinked a few times. "No."

Betty cocked her head to the side. "But you didn't even check your computer."

"We don't carry any issues from longer than a month ago," Ellen told her sweetly. *Also, I'm pretty sure that isn't a real magazine.*

"Oh," Betty sighed. She put her journal back in back into her bag. "Do you know where I could find it?"

Ellen shrugged. "Not sure. A library maybe?" *Or in some old hoarder's house.*

"That's a real shame," Betty said. "That issue brings back memories. I was working on a project inspired by it the night Raymond found out I was pregnant."

Ellen nodded. *What am I supposed to say to that?* She picked up the scanner and tried to look busy, hoping it would deter Betty from going on one of her rants. As Betty began to speak again, Ellen realized that it had failed. Again.

"I was working on one of those finger painting projects on the kitchen wall when Raymond walked into the kitchen. He seemed mad. He waved the pregnancy test from that morning in my face. 'Da fuck is this?' he cried!"

Ellen looked around. *Please let another customer be in the store and need my help.*

No such luck. "He grabbed my hand," Betty continued. "'I'ma fix dis,' he told me. He led me into the bedroom and threw me down on the bed. And he fucked me so hard that the next morning, I wasn't pregnant anymore."

Ellen stood behind the counter, dumbfounded. But Betty wasn't done.

"He literally fucked me so hard that it gave me an abortion!"

Ellen put down her scanner and came out from behind the counter. "Oh dear, Betty, would you look at the time, we're closing!"

She grabbed Betty by the shoulder and gently pushed her towards the door. Betty resisted.

"I thought you were open until 11?" she asked.

"Nope, 10:30 tonight. Sorry, manager's orders!" Ellen announced. She let go of Betty and opened the door. "Have a good night, ma'am."

Bewildered, Betty wandered out the door. The second her feet passed the threshold, Ellen shut the door behind her and locked it.

She turned around and saw her manager, a young guy with a mustache and a bad haircut, staring at her, mouth agape.

"Did you just lock the door?" her manager demanded.

Ellen pointed at Betty who was wandering around the parking lot tapping on car windows. "I began to fear for the safety of the customers and the employees," she exclaimed. *It's not a total lie.*

The manager looked out the door and watched as Betty began inspecting the tires of a pick-up truck.

"Ya know, that's not her car," the manager muttered. He patted Ellen on the back. "Good call."

C.M. GABBETT is the author of over a dozen political articles and numerous short stories. His work has appeared in *RedAlert Politics, Black Lantern Publishing, The Gambler, Section 8, The Ramapo News* and *Trillium,* among other publications. He currently lives in central New Jersey.

The Whiskey Club
Peter Jelen

"...I'm telling you he copies everything I do. Last week I showed up at The Whiskey Club in a bowler hat and tonight, guess who walks through the door wearing the exact same hat."

"You have a bowler hat? I've never seen you wear a bowler hat."

"Who cares about the bowler hat, my point is they're mental, and we're quitting the club."

"I'm not quitting just because Marshall showed up in a bowler hat."

"It's not just the bowler hat, it's everything. Remember London? Do you really think he had a conference?"

"It's easier for me to believe they went all the way to London for a conference than went there just to have dinner with us."

"Well they did. Think about it, we told them where we were staying, when we'd be there, and they didn't bother to mention that they'd be there too, at the exact same hotel, the exact same weekend!"

Amber carried her wine glass across their small kitchen and sat down next to Ben on the sofa.

"Now," she said softly, "think about what you're saying. That this 37 year old man and his wife have begun mimicking our lives just because we sat down to have a drink with them one night at The Whiskey Club."

"Amber, I know how it sounds but trust me, he's deranged. They're both deranged and I'm going to prove it."

"Prove what?"

"Hand me my phone. I'll show you what I'm talking about."

Ben wrote Marshall a text. It said:

Good to see you again old chap. Just got back home, Amber sends her hellos to you and Gretchen. See you next week brotosaurus.

He showed the message to Amber, then sent it.

"And what is this silly message going to prove exactly?"

"Wait, you'll see."

Ben's phone chirped less than a minute later. It was a text from Marshall. It read:

Good to see you too old chap. Just got back home too. Gretchen sends her regards to you and Amber. I'll save you a seat next week brotosaurus.

"See!" said Ben. "See!"

"So he copied your diction."

"It's not just the diction. It's the bowler hat, the "conference trip" to London, the alpaca scarf, my goatee. Everything."

"Leave it alone."

"I won't."

"These are the first people we've met since we moved here. It's not exactly easy to make friends in your thirties, so please, let's just give them a chance. You're always so critical! Remember Kayla and Michael? You're doing the same thing with Marshall and Gretchen."

"Was I wrong about Kayla?"

"I didn't ask if you were right or wrong, I just asked if you remembered."

"How could I forget? She divorced the guy 'cause he had cancer."

"Not just because he had cancer."

"Whatever. If you prefer blindness to vision, then by all means, go to The Whiskey Club next week. I won't be there."

***

The next Friday, just before Amber left for The Whiskey Club, Ben sent Marshall a text informing him that he wouldn't be attending this week due a case of the shits, to which Marshall promptly replied, "Me too, brotosaurus. Had some bad lamb curry for lunch."

Ben shoved the message in Amber's face, "See! See!"

"I gotta go."

"Have fun."

"I intend to."

"Wait!"

"What?"

Ben grabbed his coat out of the closet, "Since Marshall's not going tonight, that means I will."

"You're so childish." Amber closed the door.

"I'm childish because some crazy 37 year old man is copying me?" Ben hit the down button on the elevator in the hall.

"Even if he is, so what?"

"So what!"

"Yeah, so what? It's not that big a deal. If anything it's kind of flattering."

"So you admit it?"

"I'm not admitting anything. I'm just saying that if he is copying you, then you should consider it a compliment."

"I consider it frightening." The elevator dinged and the doors opened.

"Terrifying. I bet they've been using the Whiskey Club as preying ground to find couples to mimic, and once they've copied and consumed their lives they move on to the next couple."

"I didn't want to say it, Amber. But yes, that's exactly what I think! I bet their names aren't even Gretchen and Marshall. I'll wager those are the names of the couple before us!"

"You're insane."

They got out on the first floor and walked the four blocks to The Whiskey Club on 2nd Street. It wasn't anything fancy; an apartment above a Korean grocery with a few micro suede loveseats, a maroon L-shaped sofa, and a large oak cabinet with wicker shutters containing hundreds of bottles of whiskeys from locales around the world. Ben liked it here because it was one of the only places in the city where you could still sit and smoke a cigar indoors. To him, that alone was worth the annual two hundred dollar membership fee. He really didn't want to quit the club, and there were always ways to circumnavigate Marshall and Gretchen, but it wasn't something he wanted to worry about every time he showed up. Sure, he could simply stop talking to them outright; ignore them when they walked through the door, but The Whiskey Club was a small place, and when the room became tense it made being there as awkward as swimming through a lake of petroleum jelly. If he couldn't get Amber to see what Marshall was doing, or better still, get her to understand the oddity of his behavior, he would simply have to surrender, and stop going there.

He told Amber as much when they sat down next to the store windows.

"If you think he's copying you," she said, "why don't you just call him out on it?"

"And say what? I know you're copycatting me."

"Yeah."

"That's actually not a bad idea. Why should I have to quit the club because he's a psycho?"

"Although, if he is copying you, he'll probably claim you're the one copying him."

"True. But maybe he'll get so embarrassed he won't show up anymore."

"Look," said Amber, pointing down below. "Here comes Gretchen, sans Marshall."

"Thank God."

They craned their necks down and diddled their phones pretending not to notice Gretchen when she walked in. It wasn't until her shadow fell over their screens that they lifted their faces with feigned surprised and invited her to sit.

"How's Marshall?" Amber asked.

"Obviously not as well as Ben," she said.

"I'm feeling better, thanks for asking."

"You told Marshall weren't going to make it tonight."

"He's sick anyway, so what does it matter?"

Gretchen snorted, leaned back in the loveseat, covered her face with her phone and sent a clandestine text.

"Excuse me," said Amber, sliding out of her seat.

"Where're you going?" asked Ben.

"The ladies room. If that's alright with you?"

Gretchen's phone buzzed. When Ben got up to let Amber out he peeked over Gretchen's shoulder and read the text on her phone. It was from Marshall, it said, "*I'm out the door, wife-a-roni.*"

"Good news," she told Ben. "Marshall's feeling better and is on his way."

"Excellent."

"You know," said Gretchen, "the truth is Marshall wasn't really having stomach problems."

"Is that so?"

"He had surgery, and well...He shouldn't drink."

"Surgery?"

"It was elective."

"He never mentioned anything to me."

"It's kind of embarrassing."

"Oh."

"He has smegma."

"Smegma."

"You know what smegma is, don't you Ben?"

His legs trembled and his eyes twitched. He wanted to reach over the table and choke her. No. Not her. Amber. "Yes," he grumbled through gritted teeth. "I know what smegma is."

"So you know how unbearable it can be. And believe me, it was unbearable. The build up was so thick, so rank, he had no other alternative. He had to get circumcised. I couldn't even go near it. It's been nearly a year since we had sex, you know."

"Is that so?"

"Maybe I shouldn't be telling you this."

"No, you shouldn't."

"But we're all friends. All adults. Right?"

Amber saw Ben's eyes bulging and flared as she returned from the restroom. She could tell something was going on, but she wasn't prepared for this.

"What's up?"

"Oh, not much," said Ben. "Amber was just telling me about how *Marshall* had to get circumcised because of *his* intolerable smegma."

Amber's jaw dropped, "Oh."

"Excuse me."

"Ben, wait!"

He stormed into the men's room, stepped up to the urinal, closed his eyes and breathed deeply counting down from ten trying to calm him himself. He paid no attention to the door squeaking open, to the pair of feet clopping up to the urinal next to him. It wasn't until he finished relieving himself and opened his eyes that he finally saw Marshall standing beside him, staring down at his dick with big gleaming eyes and an excited smile.

"Look brotosaurus, we're twins."

Ben couldn't stop himself. He had to look at Marshall's penis, proudly being displayed in his hands like a newly won trophy. It looked like something out of a horror movie; all stitched up and bruised yellow. If Frankenstein's monster had a dick, that's what it looked it.

"Like the new hat?"

"No! No, I don't."

Ben zipped up his fly and scurried into the foyer where Amber was waiting. He pushed right past her and stomped down the stairs to the street. She followed behind him begging him to wait, but he wouldn't. It wasn't until he got stopped at a traffic light on 3rd Street that she finally caught up to him.

"Ben, wait. Listen. I'm sorry!"

"How could you?"

"I was tipsy one night and we were talking about sex. I didn't think..."

"Who else have you told?"

"No one, I swear."

"You swore you wouldn't tell anybody to begin with."

"You're partly to blame, Ben."

"Me?"

"It was your idea to join a whiskey club, what did you think would happen after I drank all that whiskey?"

"So if I get drunk I can tell people that you have a malodorous vagina."

"But I don't."

"You're missing the point."

"I said I'm sorry, what more do you want?"

"Admit it! Admit he's been copying me."

"He didn't really get circumcised; Gretchen just said that because she was angry you lied to Marshall."

"Oh yeah. Then who just accosted me at the urinal showing off his new hat?"

"What new hat?"

Ben explained the exchange with Marshall in the bathroom.

"How do you know he wasn't already circumcised?"

"I saw it! The thing still had stitches in it."

"You're messed up, Ben."

"Me?"

"You looked at his penis. Really? That's fucked up. You're the one that needs help, Ben. Not Marshall."

"Why won't you accept it, Amber?"

"You know what I accept, your egocentricity. You think you're better than everyone else. That's why you have trouble making friends. Marshall's a really nice guy, and you just had to go and find something you don't like about him."

"I'm going home."

"And I'm going back to the club."

"Fine."

"You really should do some thinking, Ben. I'm getting tired of your shit."

"Oh, I'm going to think alright." *About getting a divorce.*

"Good. I'll see you when I get home."

"Maybe I won't be there."

***

But he was. He was waiting when she stumbled through the door half past midnight and flung her purse into the bedroom, not quite drunk, not quite tipsy. "Ben! Ben," she called out.

"What?"

"Where are you?"

"Here," he stepped in from the balcony where he was enjoying a cigar.

"I'm sorry. You were right."

"So you've finally gotten your vision back."

"I'm sorry, okay."

"When did you realize it?"

"After you left they asked me why, and I straight up told them."

"You told them!"

"I'm not a child, of course I told them."

"And what did they say?"

"Marshall admitted it. He worships you, he thinks you're the coolest guy in the world, how you flip your collar up, listen to jazz music on vinyl, wear a beatnik goatee, suspenders instead of a belt, never leave the house without a pocket square. He said you're 'the bee's knees'."

"See," said Ben, "now was that so hard for you to admit?"

"Oh, and he asked me if it's alright if he can become a vegetarian too. Because its soooooo cool."

"Are you being sarcastic?"

"No," she smirked, "totally serious."

"And the circumcision, did he tell you about the circumcision?"

"He didn't go into detail, but said something about never feeling so free since he stopped wearing a turtle neck, like you."

"I told you. I told you. See! You see it now?"

"Yep, sure do. I see it now."

Whether she was being completely genuine didn't matter to Ben, she'd said it, and that was good enough for him. At least until next week.

PETER JELEN received a B.A. in English Literature from McMaster University in 2007, and expatriated to South Korea shortly after to work as an English teacher to pay off his student loans. What was supposed to be a year, ended up being seven. He has lived and worked in China, Japan, Thailand, Vietnam, Cambodia, and Indonesia. In the summer of 2015 he finally returned home to Hamilton, Ontario where he lives with his wife and cat.

Better Than God
Peter Jelen

Euthanasia is a firing squad, the Catholic Church brings the Son of Man back to life with the Shroud of Turin, doctors create imaginary mental disorders to further their careers, and God hands in his letter of resignation in the form of a suicide note while lonely young girls seek out pedophiles on the Internet just for some attention.

Better Than God is a collection of dark and humorous fast-paced imaginative stories filled with unforgettable characters only Peter Jelen can provide.

Better Than God
$12.99
6" x 9"
254 pages
ISBN-13: 978-0988075016
ISBN-10: 0988075016
BISAC: Fiction / Short Stories

Knuckle Sandwiches
Wayne F. Burke

Knuckle Sandwiches is a punch in the face to art, culture, and society. A smack in the mouth to propriety. Knuckle sandwiches of the literal kind as well as the more common, but no less painful, metaphorical kind, which life gives to everyone regardless of race, creed, class, or gender.

Knuckle Sandwiches
$14.98
5.25" x 8"
116 pages
ISBN-13: 978-1926449081
ISBN-10: 1926449088
BISAC: Poetry / General

garbageflower
Damon Ferrell Marbut

With garbageflower, Damon Ferrell Marbut demonstrates once again how each book is its own unique expression of human engagement. The generosity of this collection comes from the shared moment, wherein often Marbut leaves defining the poem's purpose up to the reader. Other times there is no doubting how firmly he believes there is no line separating abstraction from reality. This believable, touching book of poems is for everyone.

garbageflower
$15.00
5.5 x 8.5
102 pages
ISBN-13: 978-1926449074
ISBN-10: 192644907X
BISAC: Poetry / General

Heaven's Gone To Hell
Andrew J. Simpson

Heaven's Gone To Hell leads the reader through a series of humorous dystopias that challenge the way we use language and the way we see the world. From alcoholic archangels, to heaven's reliance on unpaid labour, to a devil just trying to do what's right, Andrew J. Simpson's follow-up to The Big Picture turns the tropes of society on their ears.

"The mind of Andrew J. Simpson is an ideas machine … His brain is actually a powerful alien computer."

~ *Alejandro Bustos, Apartment 613*

Heaven's Gone To Hell
$19.99
6" x 9"
174 pages
ISBN-13: 978-1926449067
ISBN-10: 1926449061
BISAC: Fiction/ General

Remote Life
Edward Anki

Remote Life slices into the reader's mind like a paper cut, provoking thought, mild discomfort, and the unsettling thrill of a direct and immediate experience of reality. In this collection of poems, Edward Anki addresses the disconnectedness of modern urban existence in raw and unforgiving terms, offering an unfiltered take on everything from the struggles of dating to the stark actualities of aging and death.

Remote Life
$10.00
5.25" x 8"
46 pages
ISBN-13: 978-1926449029
ISBN-10: 1926449029
BISAC: Poetry / General

Remote
Life

Edward
Anki

Impressions Of An Expatriate: China
Peter Jelen

Impressions Of An Expatriate is an honest, firsthand examination of one expat's experiences living in China dealing with culture shock, racism, and assimilation. From his encounters with children grown in cages to bears fighting to the death in a pit at the base of the Great Wall, Jelen's poems leave little to the imagination with haunting, vivid portraits that will take you on a trip.

"Jelen observes everything going on all around him, and as he sees it happening, he's taking it in, and becoming wise in the ways of the world…"

~ *Carl Miller Daniels*

Impressions Of An Expatriate: China
$8.50
5.25" x 8"5
60 pages
ISBN-13: 978-0992035563
ISBN-10: 0992035562
BISAC: Poetry / General

Hearing Voices
The BareBack Anthology

Since 2012 BareBack has sought to publish writers who are straightforward, sincere, and passionate. Hearing Voices: The BareBack Anthology features the most innovative and honest poetry, fiction, and flash fiction that has appeared in BareBackMagazine since its inception. Hearing Voices is bold, brave, and a great showcase of some amazingly talented new and established writers from around the world.

Hearing Voices: The BareBack Anthology
$14.99
6 x 9
132 pages
ISBN-13: 978-0992035549
ISBN-10: 0992035546
BISAC: Poetry / General

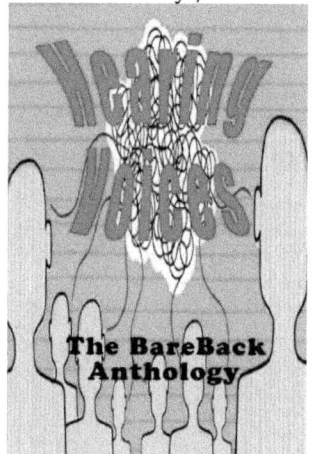

Unwrapped
The BareBack Anthology

A collection of innovative poetry from poets speckled around the world who have been featured in BareBack Magazine ~ an online publication dedicated to BareBack writers. People who aren't afraid to take off their gloves and give the world sincere, unpretentious, honest writing that has punch. Unwrapped is dark, humorous, and sometimes downright strange.

Unwrapped: The BareBack Anthology
$14.99
6" x 9"
136 pages
ISBN-13: 978-098-807-504-7
ISBN-10: 098-807-504-0
BISAC: Poetry / General

Be Kind to Strangers
Carl Miller Daniels

A wild and wondrous group of poems, BE KIND TO
STRANGERS is the most recent collection of work by Carl
Miller Daniels. Sweet, sexy, and alarming, with more than a hint
of gentle absurdism, these poems cross the paths from sadness
to joy, with a sense of awe and amazement that things in this
world, are like they are.

Be Kind to Strangers
$8.50
5.25" x 8"
56 pages
ISBN-13: 978-1926449043
ISBN-10: 1926449045
BISAC: Poetry / General

DICKHEAD
Wayne F. Burke

One of the best volumes of poetry published this year or any
year, DICKHEAD is an absurdist knuckle sandwich that deals
in realism and farce in equal measures: simultaneously a
punch to the gut and massage--jasmine mixed with hemlock--a
ride through the Tunnel of Love and into the Fun House...An
eclectic stew of poetry that engages both soul and spleen, heart
as well as mind.

Dickhead
$13.00
5.25" x 8"
108 pages
ISBN-13: 978-1926449050
ISBN-10: 1926449053
BISAC: Poetry / General

Old Gods for New
Mike Algera

Old Gods for New reflects upon personal triumphs and demons, love and longing, the past and never-was; musings that spark both the artistry of playful banter as well as lyrical madness. Writing that is quirky yet daring, combining scratch words into something new.

"Algera is a magician of poetry sometimes playful, sometimes breath-takingly revelatory. Like a stunt pilot, he drives the expected into the unexpected, in slow, deceptive circles, showing us new countries of thought, new vistas of imagery."

~Joe Girard, Author and Host of CFMU's Saturn's Rings

Old Gods for New
$14.99
6" x 9"
132 Pages
ISBN-13: 978-0992035594
ISBN-10: 0992035597
BISAC: Illustrated Poetry

Old Gods for New

Mike Algera

www.barebackpress.com

And So On...And Son On...And So On... And So On...And So
On... And So On...And Son On...And So On... And So On...And
So On...And So On...And Son On...And So On... And So
On...And So On...And So On...And Son On...And So On... And
So On...And So On...And So On...And Son On...And So On...
And So On...And So On...And So On...And Son On...And So
On... And So On...And So On...And So On...And Son On...And
So On... And So On...And So On...And So On...And Son
On...And So On... And So On...And So On...And So On...And
Son On...And So On... And So On...And So On...And So
On...And Son On...And So On... And So On...And So On...And
So On...And Son On...And So On... And So On...And So
On...And So On...And Son On...And So On... And So On...And
So On...And So On...And Son On...And So On... And So
On...And So On...And So On...And Son On...And So On... And
So On...And So On...And So On...And Son On...And So On...
And So On...And So On... And So On...And Son On...And So
On... And So On...And So On...And So On...And Son On And
So On... And So On...And So On...And So On...And Son
On...And So On... And So On...And So On...And So On...And
Son On...And So On... And So On...And So On...And So
On...And Son On...And So On... And So On...And So On...And
So On...And Son On...And So On... And So On...And So On...
And So On...And Son On...And So On... And So On...And So
On...And So On...And Son On...And So On... And So On...And
So On...And So On...And Son On...And So On... And So
On...And So On... And So On...And Son On...And So On... And
So On...And So On...And So On...And Son On...And So On...
And So On...And So On...And So On...And Son On...And So
On... And So On...And So On...And So On...And Son On...And
So On... And So On...And So On...And So On...And Son
On...And So On... And So On...And So On...And So On...And
Son On...And So On... And So On...And So On...And So
On...And Son On...And So And So On...And So On...And So
On...And Son On...And So On... And So On...And So On...And
So On...And Son On...And So On... And So On...And So On...
And So On...And Son On...And So On... And So On...And So
On... And So On...And Son On...And So On... And So On...And
So On...And So On...And Son On...And So On... And So
On...And So On...And So On...And Son On...And So On... And
So On...And So On...And So On...And Son On...And So On...
And So On...And So On...And So On...And Son On...And So
On... And So On...And So On... And So On...And Son On......
And So On...And Son On...And So On... And So On...And So

On... And So On...And Son On...And So On... And So On...And
So On...And So On...And Son On...And So On... And So
On...And So On...And So On...And Son On...And So On... And
So On...And So On...And So On...And Son On...And So On...
And So On...And So On...And So On...And Son On...And So
On... And So On...And So On...And So On...And Son On...And
So On... And So On...And So On...And So On...And Son
On...And So On... And So On...And So On...And So On...And
Son On...And So On... And So On...And So On...And So
On...And Son On...And So On... And So On...And So On...And
So On...And Son On...And So On... And So On...And So
On...And So On...And Son On...And So On... And So On...And
So On...And So On...And Son On...And So On... And So
On...And So On...And So On...And Son On...And So On... And
So On...And So On...And So On...And Son On...And So On...
And So On...And So On... And So On...And Son On...And So
On... And So On...And So On...And So On...And Son On And
So On... And So On...And So On...And So On...And Son
On...And So On... And So On...And So On...And So On...And
Son On...And So On... And So On...And So On...And So
On...And Son On...And So On... And So On...And So On...And
So On...And Son On...And So On... And So On...And So On...
And So On...And Son On...And So On... And So On...And So
On...And So On...And Son On...And So On... And So On...And
So On...And So On...And Son On...And So On... And So
On...And So On... And So On...And Son On...And So On... And
So On...And So On...And So On...And Son On...And So On...
And So On...And So On...And So On...And Son On...And So
On... And So On...And So On...And So On...And Son On...And
So On... And So On...And So On...And So On...And Son
On...And So On... And So On...And So On...And So On...And
Son On...And So On... And So On...And So On...And So
On...And Son On...And So And So On...And So On...And So
On...And Son On...And So On... And So On...And So On...And
So On...And Son On...And So On... And So On...And So On...
And So On...And Son On...And So On... And So On...And So
On... And So On...And Son On...And So On... And So On...And
So On...And So On...And Son On...And So On... And So
On...And So On...And So On...And Son On...And So On... And
So On...And So On...And So On...And Son On...And So On...
And So On...And So On...And So On...And Son On...And So
On... And So On...And So On... And So On...And Son On......
And So On...And Son On...And So On... And So On...And So

On... And So On...And Son On...And So On... And So On...And
So On...And So On...And Son On...And So On... And So
On...And So On...And So On...And Son On...And So On... And
So On...And So On...And So On...And Son On...And So On...
And So On...And So On...And So On...And Son On...And So
On... And So On...And So On...And So On...And Son On...And
So On... And So On...And So On...And So On...And Son
On...And So On... And So On...And So On...And So On...And
Son On...And So On... And So On...And So On...And So
On...And Son On...And So On... And So On...And So On...And
So On...And Son On...And So On... And So On...And So
On...And So On...And Son On...And So On... And So On...And
So On...And So On...And Son On...And So On... And So
On...And So On...And So On...And Son On...And So On... And
So On...And So On...And So On...And Son On...And So On...
And So On...And So On... And So On...And Son On...And So
On... And So On...And So On...And So On...And Son On And
So On... And So On...And So On...And So On...And Son
On...And So On... And So On...And So On...And So On...And
Son On...And So On... And So On...And So On...And So
On...And Son On...And So On... And So On...And So On...And
So On...And Son On...And So On... And So On...And So On...
And So On...And Son On...And So On... And So On...And So
On...And So On...And Son On...And So On... And So On...And
So On...And So On...And Son On...And So On... And So
On...And So On... And So On...And Son On...And So On... And
So On...And So On...And So On...And Son On...And So On...
And So On...And So On...And So On...And Son On...And So
On... And So On...And So On...And So On...And Son On...And
So On... And So On...And So On...And So On...And Son
On...And So On... And So On...And So On...And So On...And
Son On...And So On... And So On...And So On...And So
On...And Son On...And So And So On...And So On...And So
On...And Son On...And So On... And So On...And So On...And
So On...And Son On...And So On... And So On...And So On...
And So On...And Son On...And So On... And So On...And So
On... And So On...And Son On...And So On... And So On...And
So On...And So On...And Son On...And So On... And So
On...And So On...And So On...And Son On...And So On... And
So On...And So On...And So On...And Son On...And So On...
And So On...And So On...And So On...And Son On...And So
On... And So On...And So On... And So On...And Son
On..
....And So On...................

Hamilton, Ontario
Canada